SHEDDING ASH

SHEDDING ASH

SUMMER N DAWN

TRIGGER WARNINGS

IF ANY OF THE FOLLOWING MAKES
YOU FEEL UNSAFE OR AFFECTS YOUR
MENTAL HEALTH, PLEASE REFRAIN
FROM READING!
YOU AND YOUR MENTAL HEALTH MAT-
TER!
TRIGGERS:
SEX
ABUSE
VIOLENCE
PAST ABUSE
PREGNANCY
STALKING
FORCED INFERTILITY

FOR ALL THE WOMEN WHO NEED THAT EXTRA MOTIVATION TO FIND THEMSELVES.
FOR THOSE WALLFLOWERS THAT ARE BLOOMING INTO ROSES, DON'T GIVE UP; YOU WILL FIND THE ONE THAT MAKES YOU BLOOM.
FOR THOSE AFRAID OF LETTING GO OF THE PAST, LET IT BURN!

FOR AARON, NEVER LET YOUR LIGHT DIM!

FOR ASH, LET'S BURN THE WORLD TOGETHER!

TO SUNSHINE, YOU ARE MY FIRE!

Contents

TRIGGER WARNINGS v

Dedication vi

Prologue 1

1 Tara Ashley 2

2 Kass Ballentine 11

3 Corey King 32

4 Roy Boyce 38

5 Shannon 41

6 Tori Chance 53

7 Shannon 55

8 Corey 61

9 Kass 66

10 Shannon 76

11 Shannon 85

12 Corey 94

13 Roy 112

14 Shannon   115

15 Shannon   126

16 Tori   133

17 Kass   136

18 Corey   157

19 Kass   187

20 Roy   209

21 Shannon   215

22 Corey   226

23 Corey   238

24 Epilogue   243

About the Author   251

Author's Note   252

Prologue

Shannon

I escaped my former life, one in which I was nothing more than a punching bag, battered both emotionally and physically.

For five long years, I was married to a man who saw me as nothing but a vessel for his rage.

That fateful day, when Kass took Tara Ashley's life, marked a turning point that unraveled everything I once knew.

In the aftermath, Shannon Warren was born—a new identity shielded by the protective arms of the Bratva, a world steeped in shadows yet offering me a semblance of safety.

Now, four years have passed since my rebirth, and I should feel secure, yet the echoes of my past linger just beyond the horizon.

Should I fall in love or be married to my job?

1

Tara Ashley

TEN YEARS AGO

Being married to an asshole, whose ego is bigger than his dick sucks!

Roy Boyce married me just to please his father.

We got married the moment I turned 18, stepping into a new chapter of our lives.

His father had issued an ultimatum: marry or forfeit his chance to inherit the family company. It was an offer he couldn't refuse, bound by duty and expectation.

As he stood in the lively pharmacy, a cacophony of bustling footsteps and the faint rustling of prescription bottles filling the air, his gaze landed on me, an unsuspecting pharmacy technician behind the counter.

I was a swirl of activity, deftly balancing a handful of medications while managing the steady stream of customers clamoring for assistance.

My hair, pulled back into a messy bun, seemed to mirror the delightful chaos of the space around me, and my name badge, slightly askew, only added to my endearing disarray.

I was blissfully unaware of my own limits, simply caught up in the spirit of the moment and eager to help anyone in need.

We began dating in the vibrant bloom of spring, our days filled with laughter, adventures, and countless deep conversations that seemed to stretch into the night.

After six enchanting months of building memories together, we made the decision to take the next step in our journey as a couple. We exchanged vows shortly thereafter in an intimate ceremony amidst the vibrant energy of New York City. In this iconic metropolis, where dreams dance between the tall skyscrapers and bustling streets, even 17-year-olds could marry with parental consent.

The lively atmosphere not only enveloped us but also became the perfect backdrop for the beginning of our new life as husband and wife.

Initially, I thought it was true love.

Each week, I found myself pleasantly surprised by the arrival of exquisitely arranged bouquets, bursting with vibrant colors and the intoxicating scent of fresh lilies, roses, and jasmine.

Alongside these floral delights, rich boxes of artisanal chocolates beckoned with their silky ganaches and enticing flavors, a sweet indulgence to brighten my days.

However, now I feel trapped within the four familiar walls of our home, the world outside seemingly fading into obscurity. I've been forced to leave my role as a pharmacy technician, a job I cherished for its engagement with the community and the fulfillment of helping others.

Roy, my husband, became increasingly agitated by the attention I received from customers. He insisted that too many men entered the pharmacy not for their prescriptions but to flirt with me, their intentions cloaked in casual conversation. His jealousy has morphed our once vibrant lives into a suffocating prison of his making, tightening its grip with each passing day.

Despite the confinement, I find myself accepting everything he offers with a resigned heart.

The stolen kisses he gives me, filled with a surprising sweetness that lingers on my lips, are both a comfort and a reminder of the affection that once felt uninhibited.

The decadent chocolates, rich and velvety as they melt slowly in my mouth, act as a temporary salve, masking the bitter reality of my circumstances beneath layers of cacao and sugar.

The brutal beatings arrive like the clock's relentless chime, each strike a harsh reminder of my subjugation in his cruel world.

Bruises bloom across my skin like dark, painful flowers, their mottled hues a haunting testament to his twisted form of affection.

These thrashings have transformed into a daily ritual, an unyielding rhythm that reverberates through the very walls of my home. Each thud is a chilling echo of my entrapment, a sound that wraps itself around me like a suffocating shroud.

I suppose it's a small mercy that I rarely venture outside; the world beyond these confining four walls feels increasingly hostile, the mere thought of freedom rendered more daunting with every blow I endure.

As I stand in the kitchen making him his favorite meal, because it's our five-year wedding anniversary, I decided to dress up for him.

Today, I've chosen to wear a knee-length orange skirt that sways gently with each step, paired with a sleek black V-neck shirt that adds a touch of sophistication.

I selected this outfit specifically for today, as orange is my favorite color, and it always brightens my mood.

The vibrant hue of the skirt makes me feel radiant and confident, and I took the time to enhance my look with carefully applied makeup.

I can't help but hope that when Roy arrives home, he's in a cheerful mood and notices my effort. Perhaps he'll see me and be inspired to call me beautiful, bringing a smile to my face.

"Where are you, Tara?"

His booming voice echoes down the long hallway, reverberating off the walls and slicing through the stillness of the evening.

Flinching at his raised tone has now become a knee-jerk reaction, an instinct cultivated from years of practice.

The heavy clatter of utensils in the kitchen feels jarring against the backdrop of his aggression.

I take a deep breath, forcing my voice to steady as I respond, "In the kitchen, honey. I'm making spaghetti with your favorite marinara sauce. How was your day?"

I make an effort to sound cheerful, hoping it will smooth over the tension hanging in the air.

Silence stretches on, thick and uncomfortable, and just when I think he might reply, I feel the sting of his palm connect sharply with my face.

The world tilts for a moment, and I struggle to regain my balance, the taste of iron mingling with the scent of garlic and tomatoes.

"Who was here? Why are you dressed up just to cook? Who are you whoring yourself out to?"

Um, what the heck?!

"Roy, I would never do that! I dressed up for you. It's our anniversary!"

Has he lost his mind?

Roy was my first, my everything!

He thinks that I would cheat on him?

I let him beat me.

I let him use me to get off I have not once had an orgasm.

There was a time when I loved him, but now I don't know what I want.

How many more bruises will I get?

When will he just hold me again instead of tossing me aside after he gets his rocks off?

"Roy, I will never cheat on you! I don't even leave the damn house!"

BAM!

I crumbled to the ground as he punched me in the stomach.

"Watch your fucking tone with me! I own you! Everything you have is because of me! I can take it from you in an instant! I have my fortune because we are married, so I don't need you anymore. I only keep you around for appearances."

He snatches me up by my hair.

"Roy, stop it, you're hurting me!"

He grabs his pocket knife and puts it to my throat.

"Good! I will teach you your place! You belong to me! You will serve me in every way I tell you to! Right now, that is in my bed."

I squirm in his grasp.

"Honey, please! I'm sorry, but please don't do this. Don't make me suck you! Please!"

His maniacal laugh breaks my heart.

"Poor sweet, Ash! You will suck my dick until I come. At least you know what your consequences are!"

As we make it to our cold, depressing bed, he removes the knife from my throat, and he throws me on the bed.

"Strip and be a good little whore since you want to dress like one!"

I tune everything out, and my vision goes black. He won't stop until he gets what he wants.

2

Kass Ballentine

Being in New York alone is an utterly isolating experience.

I came to this bustling city in search of a significant emotional break, hoping to find some semblance of peace amidst the chaos of my life.

Being married to the head of the Bratva has both its undeniable advantages and stark drawbacks.

Right now, I find myself overwhelmed by the weight of the cons.

I know deep down that he loves me, but sometimes it feels like he longs for me to revert to the helpless version of myself that I once was—the incapable Kass I fought so hard to overcome.

Throughout my life, I've faced the challenges of living with a disability; I was gifted with a mild form of cerebral palsy because someone who was supposed to protect me decided that they needed to shake some sense into me.

Navigating through life, I've learned to accept that I walk with a noticeable, uneven gait, an ever-present reminder of my struggles. And in moments of frustration, my voice falters, giving rise to a stutter that often feels like an echo of my insecurities.

My husband, Massimo, is the Pakhan, or leader, of his crew in the bustling city of Chicago. His role involves a mix of respect and danger, as he navigates both the legitimate and illicit sides of his work.

While he has always displayed a loving and caring side—often surprising me with little acts of kindness and support—lately, those qualities seem overshadowed by the demands of his job.

It's become painfully clear that his work, whether it falls within the bounds of the law or not, takes precedence over our relationship.

Despite this struggle, I can't ignore the transformative impact he has had on me.

Through his guidance, I've become a fierce woman who knows how to defend herself, both physically and emotionally. I now find myself standing my ground and refusing to accept any disrespect from those around me, a skill I developed in part because of the world he has introduced me to.

I told him I would check on him later, but by "later," I mean months or even years.

Our son, Warren, is five years old and is oblivious to his fathers actions, but his adopted sister knows everything. She is nineteen, Tasha Ballentine, she was adopted when he was three. She understands the peculiarities of our lives, but she longs for a taste of normalcy. Whenever I have the chance to grant her that wish, I will seize it wholeheartedly.

We are careful not to burden her with our concerns. If she needs to know, Massimo will conjure up some explanation, or Tasha will learn of my absence when she reaches out for our monthly call.

Lately, Massimo has been withdrawn, his affection like a flickering candle in a dimly lit room. This growing distance has made it clear: I need this break.

It's a crucial moment for me to rediscover and nurture the love I once had for myself.

It's a rare opportunity for me to focus on my own desires and needs, free from the constant demands of others seeking my help.

New York was my top choice for a stopover before I return home to Mississippi. I know my dad would be thrilled to see me, and I'm seriously considering making that visit.

As I stroll through a tranquil neighborhood, where the soft rustle of leaves fills the air, a sudden disturbance pierces the calm.

"HAVE YOU LEARNED YOUR LESSON?"

SMACK!

The pleas grow louder, echoing off the nearby houses.

"Yes, honey! I'm sorry, I won't do it again!"

"WHAT WOULDN'T YOU DO, WHORE?"

I can hardly believe he's addressing someone in such a manner!

"I will not wear bright or low-cut clothes without asking for permission."

SMACK!

"WHAT ELSE?"

Her whimpers escalate into full sobs, a haunting sound that grips my heart.

"I will remember my place and the consequences I will face if I do not obey my husband!"

Excuse me?

What kind of brainwashing is this?

We are not regressing to some archaic era—women today are empowered to be strong and confident, whether or not they have a man in their life.

"THAT'S MY GOOD LITTLE WHORE."

"Yes, honey. I will do better."

He finally stops yelling.

"I am glad we have an understanding. I will be back later, I have business to finish. Clean up this mess, I won't be home until tomorrow."

"Yes, Roy."

BINGO!

I have a name!

Roy walks out of the small, cramped house only to catcall me before leaving!

"Walk that fine ass over here, I'll pull the stick out of your ass and put something else up there."

I smile in his direction, "Is that right?"

I say with full twang.

"Oh, you have an accent? That's cute, darling."

"Cute naw, deadly yes."

I flash my knife and taser.

"Oh, umm. Excuse me!"

He sprints down the street. That's what I thought, a coward who likes to control and demean women.

I only like it when I ask for it in bed; any other time, men must recognize me for the powerhouse that I am.

I pick up my phone, a sleek model with a cracked screen from last week's mishap, and dial our ever-reliable IT guy.

"Yes, my Queen? How might I assist you today?" he answers, his tone dripping with mock formality.

I can't help but chuckle, "Cut the theatrics, Corey. I need a fast background check. I just sent you the address via text. I need it done in five minutes, fully detailed. I want everything you can dig up on the man and the woman living there. Text me the findings as soon as you have them."

"A pleasure doing business with you, as always, Your Highness," he replies, the grin audible through the phone.

"Corey, for the love of all that's good, just focus on the job and spare me the commentary!"

He chuckles, "Yes, ma'am. I know you've only been out of town for a few days, but trust me—the boss is really feeling your absence."

I let out an exasperated sigh, "Good. Just make sure you don't get sidetracked. I need this information, and I need it fast."

"On it! I'll send the details over shortly, no distractions."

I disconnect, shaking my head but smiling. Massimo's men, intimidating as they may be with their imposing frames and fierce reputations, always show a softer side when it comes to our team. They might be part of the Bratva—a world wrapped in shadows—but they know loyalty and camaraderie run deep.

I just wish Massimo would let his guard down a bit more. There's so much I want to see beneath that tough exterior.

My phone chimes softly, pulling me from my thoughts, and I eagerly glance at the screen where all the details await.

As I carefully sift through the information, a rush of anger and protectiveness runs through me.

I'm going to need backup.

Feeling the urgency in my gut, I dial Jared, my go-to guy, and listen to the rings echo through the air. He finally picks up on the third ring, his voice laced with playful sarcasm.

"Your majesty! How can I assist you today? Missing him already?"

I roll my eyes, irritation bubbling beneath the surface at the overly curious Bratva men who seem to be everywhere these days.

"I plead the fifth! I need Arson in New York ASAP! I've got a job that can't wait another day. How soon can you get here?"

He chuckles softly, the sound a mix of amusement and camaraderie. "Drop me a pin and tell me a time. I've been in New York since you arrived. Sara is with me; he didn't want you to be alone in this hectic city."

Damn it, Massimo! He always thinks ahead, and I just want to focus on the task at hand.

Damn, Jared, too, with his unwavering loyalty that ties us all together like an invisible thread.

"Okay, enough with the sappiness, big guy! I'm glad you both are here. I'm going to need Sara's connections—she knows this city like the back of her hand."

I quickly sent him a pin to my location, and the map glowing on my screen showed my exact coordinates.

"Meet me here in thirty minutes. Shoot me a text when you arrive, just in case I'm still tied up with my current situation."

With that, I hang up, readying myself for the emotional roller coaster that is about to unravel.

Tara Ashley

My makeup is tarnished, smudged like a forgotten masterpiece, each streak on my face telling a story of despair, while the bruises begin to bloom across my body—a vivid, painful reminder of the events that unfolded throughout the night.

Why me?

Why on our anniversary, a day specifically set aside to honor our love and the memories we've built together?

Is this truly how he sees me—as nothing more than a mere object, a discarded trinket that he can mistreat, a whore who would betray him and shatter the vows we once held sacred?

I have never been unfaithful; all I crave is to escape this living hell. Gone is the man that Roy used to be, thoughtful, considering, and loving. All that remains is the monster and his chains that suffocate and bind. I can't continue like this. I don't deserve this; I deserve happiness, too.

I need to break free from these suffocating chains—my spirit cries out for liberation.

I can't continue living in this turmoil; I deserve the chance to be happy once more.

A soft knock echoes from the back door, pulling my attention sharply from the dimly lit kitchen. The clock on the wall ticks ominously, its relentless march proclaiming the late hour. Who could possibly be in my backyard at this time? The streetlights outside cast long shadows, and an unsettling chill creeps into the air.

Should I feel scared?

No. I refuse to give in to fear.

No one could inflict more pain on me than Roy already has, and I've learned to brace myself against the unknown.

With a deep breath, I slowly unlock the door, the metal handle cold beneath my fingers.

I only crack it open, allowing just enough space to see who dares to intrude. I focus my gaze on the ground, avoiding direct eye contact as a precaution. "How can I help you? I didn't order anything. Why are you in my backyard?" My voice trembles slightly, revealing an edge of uncertainty.

My eyes flicker to the shoes of the person standing on my porch—royal blue pumps, sleek and eye-catching against the backdrop of the weathered wooden steps.

A woman!

My heart races at the thought that Roy might have given a woman our address.

"If you're here for Roy, he went back to work late. I'm sorry," I manage to say, trying to keep my tone steady.

She responds in a soft yet commanding voice, the kind that holds an unexpected authority, "I am here for you, Tara."

I open the door fully now, curiosity piqued despite my reservations, and look her in the eyes. The moment is electric. This woman is breathtaking—long, wavy hair cascading over her shoulders, striking features highlighted by the moonlight, and an air of confidence that draws me in.

"Why? And how do you know my name?" I ask, my heart pounding, torn between intrigue and caution.

"I will explain everything," she says, her voice warm and inviting despite the chill in the air. "But can I come in before the neighbors discover I am here? I assure you, I am not here to harm you. I am here to offer you a new life if you want it."

The sincerity in her eyes is compelling, leaving me grappling with the gravity of her words as I weigh my options.

"Fine. Please come in," I finally relent, still guarded. "But I won't guarantee that I will agree to your plan. I'm listening."

"My name is Kassani Carter, but you can call me Kass. I devote my life to rescuing women from terrible situations just like yours. I genuinely want to help you. I overheard the tense exchange between you and Roy, and believe me, you do not deserve to be treated that way. I've done my homework on him—I have my resources. Did you know he has multiple girlfriends? I gathered all the proof—it's right here on my phone."

I take a cautious glance at her device, my heart racing. The screen floods with naked pictures of Roy alongside various women, and my stomach churns as tears silently trail down my face.

"How recent are those?" I stammer, feeling a mix of disbelief and anger.

Kass lets out a heavy sigh, her expression serious. "These are a week old. But that's not all. My IT guy managed to hack into his apartment camera; I can show you live footage right now. He is cheating on you as we speak, Tara."

"What? No, that can't be true! He said he had to work. You need to show me this—I don't believe you!" My voice trembles with denial, clinging desperately to the hope that I might be wrong.

With a determined look, Kass taps a button on her phone, and suddenly, Roy fills the entire screen.

His voice reverberates through the room like an unwelcome echo. "She has no idea I am here, baby. And even if she did, I wouldn't care. Do you like the apartment I bought for us? You can decorate it however you like."

As he caresses the other woman's face, the intimacy of his touch stabs at my heart. Why isn't he like that with me? The contrast between his tender affection for her and the cold indifference he shows me shatters something deep inside.

I take a deep breath, trying to gather my racing emotions, and ask, "You heard our encounter from earlier?"

Kass nods, her expression serious.

"That has been my life since we got married," I continue, my voice trembling slightly. "There's been no affection, only relentless abuse, and I've been nothing more than a tool for his sexual gratification. He even forced me to undergo a hysterectomy before we exchanged vows, stripping away my dreams of motherhood—dreams I once cherished deeply.

Now, there are no children involved, no matter how much I used to yearn for them. The emotional pain and torment are suffocating, and I can't endure it any longer! I want out! How can you guarantee that you can set me free from this nightmare?"

Kass chuckles softly, but there's an edge to her voice as another knock echoes at my back door, sharp and insistent.

"My team is here," she says, glancing momentarily at the door. "Are you ready to die?"

Kass

I cast one last glance at Tara's house, now a vivid blaze against the night sky. Flames licked at the wooden beams, crackling and hissing as they devoured everything in their path. The glow illuminated the surrounding trees, casting eerie shadows that danced across the ground.

We had executed our plan with precision, sneaking Tara out just moments before we set the place ablaze. The thrill of adrenaline surged through me as I watched the fire roar to life, turning memories into ashes.

Roy would be alerted soon enough that the house was engulfed in flames. I couldn't help but feel a mix of excitement and dread.

This chaotic masterpiece was the brainchild of Jared, the only person I trusted to kindle the flames with precision and artistry. His legendary skill with fire was rivaled only by his penchant for theatrics, a combination that promised to deliver a message as loud and vivid as the blaze itself.

As the investigators sift through the aftermath, they will discover a charred figure, eerily reminiscent of Tara, dressed in the same outfit she wore this fateful night. However, the blaze will have rendered the body unrecognizable, a haunting testament to the inferno's destructive beauty.

I tap my phone screen, my heart pounding, as I watch Roy's face transform upon receiving the call informing him that his house is engulfed in flames.

Initially, he wears a carefree smile, a stark contrast to the storm brewing within him. As he disentangles himself from the arms of his girlfriend, the weight of the police officer's words slowly sinks in, twisting his happy demeanor into one of disbelief and horror.

"What did you just say? My home? What about my wife?" Roy's voice trembles, panic creeping in.

Though I can't hear the officer's voice, the anguish etched on Roy's face narrates the tragedy unfolding. His expression collapses, a mix of fear and despair as he sinks to the polished wooden floor, tears streaming down his cheeks like a torrential downpour. "Are you sure? She can't be dead! How did the fire start?" His voice is barely above a whisper, each word laced with desperation.

His girlfriend, a petite brunette with worried eyes, instinctively reaches to comfort him, but he recoils, pushing her away. The emotional weight is suffocating for him. "The oven caused the house to burn down? A faulty wire? How could we not have seen any signs before?" Panic flashes in his eyes as he grapples with the absurdity of it all, his mind racing with thoughts of what could have been.

"Yes, officer, I will make my way to the house. I'll be there in ten minutes," he responds, his voice quivering with a shaky resolve, even as the world around him feels like it's collapsing into chaos.

He has brought this on himself for the way he mistreated Tara—abuse should never be tolerated.

I'm relieved that I was able to rescue Tara from that nightmare.

She's waiting for me at the airfield, joined by Jared and Sara, as we prepare to leave for Mississippi.

Sara has meticulously arranged for Tara to undergo a complete transformation; after this, no one will recognize her. Meanwhile, Jared has reached out to Corey to secure new documents for Tara.

In just a few days, Tara will no longer exist in her current form—Shannon Warren will emerge from the shadows, ready to embrace a fresh start.

Shannon Warren

6 Weeks Later...

Six weeks ago, I left my previous life behind, marking the end of my existence as Tara Ashley.

In a calculated move orchestrated by Kass and her formidable team, the old me was discarded, paving the way for the emergence of Shannon Warren.

Kass, a woman of immense power and influence—known as the Bratva Queen—holds the reins of Chicago's underbelly, yet she has chosen this quiet corner of Mississippi to carve out her own identity. After her marriage to Massimo faded into neglect, she needed a fresh start, a chance to rediscover the woman she wants to be.

As she embarks on this journey, Kass is manifesting her dream by launching a nightclub and an exclusive sex club. Yet amidst her ambitious plans, her fierce commitment to women's empowerment shines through; she has vowed never to let another woman be reduced or diminished, which is why she rescued me.

Roy, believing me dead, will never discover that I'm alive and rebuilding. I witnessed his façade of sorrow from afar as he buried the version of me he thought he lost—he stood at my funeral, a picture of heartache, but I know all too well that his grief was fleeting. By now, he is likely back in the arms of his girlfriend or has already moved on to someone new, while my absence hardly registers in his mind.

In a month, I will begin my self-defense training, a crucial step toward reclaiming my strength and independence. Kass has offered me a position at her new club, envisioning a friendship blossoming between me and the head bartender. Her name is Tori Sullivan, a woman whose life has been marred by struggles similar to mine, yet Kass believes we can support each other and thrive in this new chapter.

Right now, I need a solid support system more than ever as I navigate this drastic transformation. I am acclimating to my thoroughly reconstructed body—a result of extensive body surgery that has turned my previous appearance into something almost unrecognizable.

My hair has undergone a radical change as well, shifting from bright blonde to a rich dark brown with burnt orange tips that reflect my newfound vibrancy. No longer the timid wallflower I once was, I'm ready to step into the spotlight with confidence, a transformation that extends beyond the surface.

Perhaps my most dramatic change is in my figure; transitioning from a B cup to a voluptuous double D has been nothing short of exhilarating—and, admittedly, a little overwhelming. These new curves are heavy, both physically and metaphorically, but they symbolize my rebirth and the woman I am destined to become.

The only thing that is the same is my ocean colored eyes.

I truly hope that one day Kass and Massimo find their way back to each other, but in the meantime, I'm eagerly anticipating the wild adventures awaiting us at the club.

I feel as though I'm transforming into a phoenix, ready to rise anew.

Let the ashes of the past burn away, making way for vibrant possibilities to unfold as my journey takes flight.

3

Corey King

PRESENT DAY..

Mississippi, really?!

Massimo has made the bold decision to tighten security at Kastaways now that Kass has transferred ownership of the club to Tori.

I can see that Massimo is thrilled to have his Queen back in Chicago, but that doesn't justify shipping off his favorite IT guy to the Sip!

He wants me to remain here for at least a few years to ensure the club is fully secure.

Like many in the Bratva, I owe the Pakhan my life and unwavering loyalty.

Before Massimo came into my life, I was nothing more than an orphan, wandering the unforgiving streets, scavenging through dumpsters for scraps just to survive.

The alleyways of Chicago are no sanctuary for the weak. I was teetering on the edge of despair, and it was Massimo who found me and reignited my will to live and thrive.

It was under his guidance that my passion for computers and cybersecurity blossomed.

He dedicated countless evenings to help me study, ensuring I had access to resources and financial support to obtain my degrees.

Now, I stand as one of the most sought-after IT professionals in the world, yet my loyalty to him surpasses any temptation of greed.

I will only work for those whom Massimo approves, as his trust and support have forged the foundation of my future.

Massimo has been an unwavering pillar of support in my life, never faltering even as I openly embraced my identity as a bisexual individual. Throughout my journey, he has been a steadfast companion, witnessing my exploration during a vibrant and adventurous chapter filled with a whirlwind of diverse experiences and connections.

During this time, I navigated the lively streets of Chicago, indulging in fleeting romances and passionate encounters, yet Massimo remained unfazed, his loyalty unshakeable.

He established one simple rule: never to encroach upon what was his. In return, he respected the choices I made, whether they were of a sexual nature or not, allowing me the freedom to explore while knowing my heart and trust were anchored to him.

Kass built Kastaways from a blend of spite and love, driven by a desire to reclaim her independence after feeling neglected.

Massimo, her partner, was often preoccupied with managing his businesses and overseeing his men, leaving Kass to fend for herself emotionally.

Recognizing the need for a change, Kass embarked on a journey across the United States, seeking clarity and purpose.

After months of travel, she found herself drawn back to her roots in Mississippi, where her father resided. It was here that she envisioned Kastaways—a sanctuary designed to provide support for those in need while also serving as a vibrant nightclub and an exclusive elite sex club.

Kastaways operates on different levels: anyone can walk into the welcoming top level to receive a hot meal or clothing without any questions asked. This tier reflects Kass's commitment to community welfare. However, level two is accessible only through membership, where patrons can enjoy a more sophisticated and exhilarating nightlife experience.

Level three is shrouded in exclusivity, reserved for a select few who meet strict criteria, adding an element of intrigue and danger.

The decision to incorporate a quaint white chapel into a kink club might seem unconventional. Still, Kass, embodying the spirit of a sweet yet formidable Bratva Queen, understood the importance of creating a space that could embrace both the sacred and the sensual.

She built Kastaways single-handedly, relying on her own savings rather than Massimo's resources. With determination and resilience, she assembled a diverse team to help run the club, marking a transition from doing everything herself to leading a collaborative effort.

Her journey from solitude to creating a thriving community hub is a testament to her strength and vision, as Kastaways evolves into a transformative space for all who enter.

I have always embraced my sexuality without hesitation. I am clear about my desires and the moments that inspire them.

For me, gender holds no significance; my heart has proudly identified as bisexual for as long as I can remember, transcending traditional boundaries.

My first love exited my life during a crucial juncture as I was navigating the complexities of pursuing my degrees. She mirrored the insecurities I had once felt with Kass, but unlike Kass, she lacked the fervor to uplift and nurture my dreams. Her priorities were firmly rooted in the practicalities of financial stability and security, overshadowing any passion for a more spirited life.

I have embraced a solitary existence for over four years now, as fleeting flings and romantic entanglements have lost their allure. Instead, I have immersed myself completely in my work, channeling my energy and ambition into building a future without distractions.

Thanks to my efforts, no one can breach Massimo's elaborate security system at Ballentine Inc. or infiltrate the intricate firewall protecting the Bratva clubhouse.

Now, I am determined to make Kastaways just as impenetrable, allowing me the freedom to unwind and savor the serene landscapes of Mississippi.

4

Roy Boyce

I am slowly reclaiming my sense of self after the profound loss of my wife, Tara, who tragically passed away four long years ago.

The pain of her absence still lingers, and I find solace in visiting her grave regularly, where I can feel close to her memory.

Our family's dynamics were strained in the wake of her passing. My father, in his grief and anger, directed his blame towards me, insisting that if I hadn't been distracted by my so-called "whores," Tara would still be alive.

To him, my relationships with other women were unforgivable distractions. He claimed to have approved of Tara, but my girlfriends never met his standards.

Two years ago, my father lost his battle with colon cancer, and with his passing came a hefty estate.

He left me everything: his successful company, his large, imposing house, and all the wealth he had meticulously saved over the years. However, I felt tethered to anything but freedom. I sold both the company and the house to Cornelis Chance, a man of considerable influence. I craved a life unburdened by the weight of a corporate job or the responsibilities of maintaining a home.

Cornelis became a mentor of sorts, drawing me into his world of power and intrigue. He assigned me tasks that, while morally dubious, provided a thrill I hadn't felt in years. I became adept at silencing women seeking to expose him, and our twisted partnership deepened as I helped him eliminate their threats—a dark yet exhilarating game.

Now, I find myself on a new mission, fueled by a sense of revenge.

We received news recently that Cornelis had passed away six months prior, his death concealed until now for reasons yet unknown. His only legitimate heir, a man named CC or Connor Chance, is currently living in Mississippi.

With only a photograph and a name to guide me, I am preparing to journey south to discover the truth about him and whatever secrets his father left behind.

The quest for answers—and justice—begins now.

5

Shannon

S afe.

Five years have slipped by since I found myself enveloped in the comforting safety net of Kastaways, a vibrant refuge that feels like home more than any place I've known.

No pain.

No abuse.

No fading into the shadows of neglect.

At Kastaways, I am truly seen and genuinely cared for in a way that revitalizes my spirit. The warm smiles and supportive words from both the compassionate staff and my fellow members serve as an uplifting balm for my past wounds.

Here, I am no longer an invisible figure weighed down by sadness but someone who is embraced for who I am—flaws, stories, and all.

Each day is an invitation to share my journey, to reflect on my growth, and to blossom in an atmosphere where kindness and understanding thrive, like the vibrant flowers in a sunlit garden.

In this sanctuary, I've rediscovered my strength, finding not just survival but a flourishing existence.

I serve as a bartender on the lively second floor, surrounded by the cheerful clinks of glasses and lively chatter that fills the air. Under the watchful guidance of Tori, the proud new owner of Kastaways, I've gained invaluable skills and deepened connections with those around me.

Just a few months ago, Kass, the former owner, made a heartfelt decision to pass the reins to Tori, allowing her the space to flourish while rekindling her own love for Massimo, the man who once pulled away from her heart.

Massimo, having experienced the void left by Kass's absence, has finally come to recognize the depth of her strength, intelligence, and the unwavering love she offered him. He understands that if he doesn't give her the consistent attention she deserves—listening to her dreams, celebrating her successes, and cherishing their shared moments—he risks losing her for good.

Their relationship stands as a beautiful testament to the love, respect, and understanding we all deserve in our lives and our connections with others. It reminds me that healing starts with the bonds we nurture, the empathy we offer, and the safe havens we create together.

It is four o'clock in the afternoon, and a soft hum of activity fills the air as we prepare to open the doors of the club.

I stand with my back to the room, intently focused on organizing the bar—a calming ritual that helps me center my thoughts and mentally brace for the evening's crowd.

The clinking of glassware and the subtle scent of citrus and herbs create a familiar atmosphere, evoking a warm, almost comforting embrace.

Suddenly, a warm, sensual voice breaks through my concentration, smooth as silk. "Excuse me, Shannon. How are you today? I'm not trying to startle you."

I pivot slowly, and my breath catches in my throat as I take in the sight of a truly striking man. Standing at six feet tall, he exudes a commanding presence, and his thick, silver-grey hair frames a chiseled face that radiates confidence. A charming smile plays upon his lips, inviting and disarming all at once.

Goodness, those muscles!

His well-defined chest, alluringly visible through a stylish fitted shirt, hints at both strength and grace, a perfect blend of masculinity. But it's his mesmerizing green eyes that truly captivate me—rich and vibrant, sparkling with a warmth and curiosity that seems to see right through me.

I'm utterly hooked—and how does he know my name?

Swoon!

"Shannon, get it together!" I silently chastise myself, feeling a flush creep across my cheeks.

Tori had mentioned she would be bringing someone in today—could this breathtaking man be him?

Don't be rude; get out of your own head and respond!

"Oh! Hello! No need to worry at all. I presume you arrived with a key? Are you the one Tori has been eagerly anticipating? Are you Corey?"

His smile broadens, a warm, inviting curve that lights up his expressive eyes. "Yes, that's me! I'll be here for a while, focused on updating the club's security systems, along with a few other tasks that Tori has entrusted to me. I genuinely look forward to collaborating with you. By the way, has anyone ever told you that you radiate such authentic compassion? You have a remarkable ability to make people feel welcome and completely at ease. Just speaking with you makes all my worries drift away. And I must add, you are truly stunning. I hope you're fully embracing this new version of yourself. Never let anyone dim your brilliance."

His words envelop me like a soft, gentle breeze, stirring a mix of excitement and disbelief within me.

"Thank you for such kind words. They truly mean a lot to me. I also want to express my heartfelt gratitude for the new identity you've helped me embrace. Kass mentioned your significant role in facilitating this transformation, and I genuinely appreciate it. I trust you're aware of my past—there's quite a bit to unravel there. I'm adjusting well, although it hasn't been a rapid journey. Gaining confidence in my new appearance poses its challenges, but I'm steadily finding my footing. I genuinely look forward to our future collaborations; your insights and support are invaluable to me. Please don't let our conversation delay you! I heard from Tori that you have the freedom to explore, so if there's anything I can assist you with, just let me know."

He tilts his head slightly to the side, allowing a warm, genuine smile to spread across his face, illuminating his features. "If you could show me that beautiful smile again, I think I'll be set for eternity," he says, his voice smooth and playful.

I let out a soft giggle, my curiosity piqued by his charming confidence. "Mr. Corey, how old are you?" I ask, intrigued.

He casually shrugs, the corners of his lips curling into a mischievous smile that lights up his eyes. "I'm forty. But I know you're almost thirty and flirty."

Wow, what a line! It sent a warm rush through me, a delightful tingling sensation radiating from my toes all the way to my fingertips, awakening a flutter of excitement within.

"Mr. Corey, I am only a mere twenty-seven. But I only flirt with those I genuinely like," I respond, my heart racing slightly as I meet his gaze. "You happen to be one of those people, and I think it's because I have nothing to hide. You know my past; I've laid the weight of it out in the open. Now, you can get to know me without rehashing all the trauma. If you're open to it, I would love to explore our friendship further with you. I keep my circle incredibly small after everything I've been through, but since Tori and Kass trust you, I feel I can, too." I pause for a moment, contemplating my next words. "Your age doesn't faze me; you're seasoned and carry a wealth of life experience. I've always felt somewhat sheltered, and maybe we can teach each other a thing or two."

He extends his hand toward me, his enthusiasm infectious, as his eyes sparkle with possibility. "Let's shake on it. To new friendships and new flirty adventures!"

With excitement bubbling inside me like a fizzy drink, I grasp his hand firmly, feeling the warmth and strength in his grip. "To adventures!" I exclaim, a smile breaking across my face.

I've never been the kind of girl to seek out exploration or spontaneity, but with him by my side, I feel a newfound courage sparking within me. Together, I'm ready to embrace the wilderness that lies ahead!

Roy

At 5:00 p.m., the atmosphere in this club is already electric, filled with a lively crowd that buzzes with anticipation.

I'm currently perched on the top level, where I've been eavesdropping on the conversations of fellow attendees. They mention that to access the second level, one must pay a membership fee. Curiously, it seems there's no background check required for those willing to fork over the fee—a policy that raises some eyebrows in terms of security. However, for me personally, that's rather fortunate.

With a sense of purpose, I make my way over to the bar, where I spot a charming redhead serving drinks. She exudes a professional demeanor, and with a friendly smile, she facilitates the payment of my membership fee without a hitch.

The top floor offers a straightforward nightclub experience, with its standard fare of upbeat music, dancing, and a live band. It's lively but lacks the exclusivity that the second level promises.

Rumors have been circulating that Connor and his little girlfriend, or whatever she is, often hang out in this building. Intrigued, I've decided to see what the second floor has to offer; after all, it can't be much in the middle of Mississippi.

As I make my way toward the elevator, I spot a cute girl waiting to board as well. She has striking brown hair with vibrant orange tips—a rather unusual combination that instantly catches my eye. Part of me thinks that someone like her needs a bit of guidance on how to present herself; I believe women should always maintain a polished appearance. Tattoos or wild hair colors can be distracting, but I have to admit that the colors in her hair don't diminish her appeal.

Her figure is certainly what I find appealing: voluptuous and curvaceous, just my type.

Before I have a chance to fully assess her, she turns slightly and speaks up, her voice soft yet firm, "Are you heading to the second floor? If so, I need to see your bracelet before I can let you on the elevator." There's a hint of confidence in her demeanor that piques my interest even further.

I gently reach around to retrieve my bracelet, the cool metal glimmering slightly in the soft light of the room.

"Thank you. You can head down with me," I say, hoping to convey my gratitude.

As she hears my words, she finally lifts her gaze to meet mine. In that fleeting moment, her entire demeanor shifts—her posture relaxes, and a hint of warmth creeps into her expression.

"Oh, um. Go ahead on down, sir! Seems I left something up here. Enjoy!" she stammers, her voice becoming oddly flustered.

I take a step toward the elevator, glancing back just as she turns and hurriedly walks away, her footsteps echoing softly against the polished floor.

Those piercing eyes!

Why do they seem so familiar?

They are mesmerizing, the kind that captivate you instantly, drawing you in like a moth to a flame, igniting an unexplainable longing to linger in that intoxicating gaze forever.

Why do those eyes seem to delve into the depths of my non-existent heart, stirring something within me that I didn't realize was still there?

Shannon

"Breathe, Shannon, breathe!"

I take a moment to steady myself before reaching for my phone, my heart pounding in my chest as I dial Tori's number. It rings just once before she answers, her voice a comforting beacon amid the chaos.

"Tore, I desperately need you to come work the bar with me. I'm about to head back down there now, but first, I have to call Kass. Roy is in the club, and I can't bear the thought of tending the bar alone with him around. I don't think he's spotted me yet, but the last thing I want is for him to. I plan to keep my distance from him. I'm not spiraling as much as I thought I would, but I'm still a bundle of nerves."

Tori's voice flows through the phone, soothing and reassuring. "Breathe. We love you, and we'll keep you safe. I'll call Kass the moment we hang up. Leave the rest to me. Corey will sit with you at the bar tonight—you won't be working. You're going to relax, enjoy a drink, and let us handle the rest. Just text me what Roy is wearing so we can keep a close eye on him."

I draw in a deep breath, feeling a wave of relief wash over me. "Okay, getting wasted sounds like the perfect plan. I'll be down shortly."

A sense of calm begins to settle over me. I trust Tori and Kass to take control of the situation. I can only hope that Roy decides to leave soon. He's the last person I want in my life right now.

As far as I'm concerned, I am completely dead to him—and I intend to keep it that way.

6

Tori Chance

Where the hell is Roy thinking by showing up at my club? This is exactly what I was afraid of.

I need to warn Kass about this chaos brewing.

Ring.

Ring.

Ring.

"Yes, my love?" Kass's soothing voice cuts through my anxiety like a warm knife through butter.

"Roy is here at Kastaways. Who knows what kind of trouble he's planning? He somehow managed to pay the membership fee and gain access to the second floor. I gave

Shannon the night off, and she's probably going to go wild at the bar with Corey. What precautionary measures should we take?"

"Did you take that class and get the certificate?"

Oh no, I see where she's headed, and my heart sinks.

"Maybe. Why do you ask?"

"You know exactly why. Hand them each two Heart of Chances! That way, you can marry Corey and Shannon tonight! I want to see it all unfold. I'll be there first thing in the morning to celebrate!"

Did she really just hang up on me?

Damn it, Kass! Why does she always pull this stunt?

Fine!

The Queen has spoken, I suppose. It looks like a Bratva marriage is on the agenda for tonight.

7

Shannon

(AT THE SECOND LEVEL BAR)

"**S**o you're my babysitter for the night?"

Corey slowly puts his hulking arm around my shoulders, "Yes, and you are my fire."

I chuckle, "Are you throwing it back to those days? Or are you referencing my hair?"

"You have me pegged, Spitfire."

I bat my eyelashes, "Have you been pegged, Junk Drive?"

"It's a jump drive, not a junk drive, and yes, I have."

Interesting.

"So let's be open, what's your sexuality? What are your dos and don'ts?"

Let's see how much he will open up to me since he knows all about my past.

"Hey squatters! Drink these!" Tori called out with a playful grin as she placed four shimmering glasses of the vibrant red Heart of Chances in front of us. "You're not allowed to move from your spots at the bar until you each finish two drinks. Enjoy!" With a mischievous wink directed at me, she added, "Shan, don't do anything I wouldn't," before skipping off, her laughter echoing through the lively pub.

I shot her a mock glare and flipped her the bird, annoyance mixing with amusement. Tori was giving me grief because I had playfully ribbed her and her husband, Connor, earlier in the evening.

As I glanced at the drinks, my mind wandered to the fact that these potent concoctions were modeled after the perfect blend of Tori and Connor's whirlwind romance—sweet with a spicy kick, just like their relationship.

Despite being four months along in her pregnancy, Tori's energy was infectious. She glided through the buzzing crowd, her blonde curls bouncing as she moved. Her demeanor was so carefree that you'd hardly guess she was expecting. There were no mood swings or fatigue for her; instead, she exuded bursts of latent energy, as if she was thriving on the excitement all around us.

"We are about to get sloshed," she said with a mischievous grin, waving the neon-colored cocktail in her hand that seemed to glow under the club's pulsating lights. "She gave us the strongest drink in the club."

I just shake my head in disbelief, feeling the anticipation building in my chest. Taking a sip of the vibrant, sweet concoction, I can already taste the rush of flavors—tropical fruit mingling with the sharpness of alcohol. I can feel it igniting the playful, flirty side of me that I usually keep tucked away. The music thumps softly in the background, the bass pulsing in time with my racing heart as I let myself be swept away by the moment.

Tori
(2 hours later)

Shannon and Corey are reveling in an utterly blissful moment, reminiscent of carefree teenagers. Their laughter rings through the air, loud and infectious, as they flirt playfully, a bit unsteady on their feet from the drinks they've shared.

Having polished off all four colorful cocktails, it's now time to unleash our plan.

"Hey, you silly gooses! Who's up for a game?" I call out, my voice bubbling with excitement.

Shan's eyes sparkle with mischief and affection as she turns to me. "I'm game!" Her gaze flits to Corey, a teasing grin spreading across her face. "How about you, Junk Drive?"

He rolls his eyes with an exasperated sigh. "It's jump drive! But sure, I can indulge a little. What's the game?"

I can't help but smirk at the playful banter. "We're diving into a classic: spin the bottle, truth or dare! Shan, you're up first!"

Her face lights up with anticipation, and she gives the bottle a spirited spin. It spins wildly for a moment before halting, pointing directly at me.

"Truth or dare, Tore?" Her giggle bursts forth, a delightful sound that dances in the air.

I can't resist smiling back. "Truth!"

Her laughter fades into a curious grin. "Is it true that you and Connor know who the baby's real father is?"

Whoa, talk about going straight for the jugular!

But honesty prevails, even knowing that the alcohol might blur the edges of their memories. "Yes, it's true. Connor is not the biological father; Spence is. But we will carry forth everything we do in his memory, and the baby will know Spence's story. We'll never place that in the shadows. As far as we're concerned, the baby has two dads."

"That's sweet, Tore," Shan smiled, her eyes sparkling with mischief.

I shrugged, a grin creeping across my face. "I guess it's my turn."

With a steady hand, I gave the bottle a careful spin on the polished wooden floor. It whirled dramatically before gradually slowing down, finally landing perfectly between Shannon and Corey.

"Well, well," I said, my voice laced with enthusiasm, "looks like this one is for both of you. Truth or dare?"

They exchanged a quick glance, a spark of excitement flaring between them, then chimed in unison, "Dare!"

I couldn't help but smirk—this was going to be fun.

"I dare you to get married," I declared, gesturing dramatically toward the corner of the room where a small, makeshift chapel was set up, complete with a lace-adorned altar and flickering candles. "Right here, right now, in my little chapel!"

Their eyes widened in surprise, and for a split second, the room fell silent, the air thick with anticipation.

8

Corey

Ouch!

Why does my head ache so intensely? It feels like a relentless throbbing pulse, as if a freight truck plowed right through me.

The pain radiates from my temples and makes it difficult to concentrate on anything else. I feel a heaviness in my forehead, and every minor sound seems to amplify the discomfort.

I roll over, feeling the plushness of a soft bed beneath me. The sheets are smooth and cool against my skin, oddly comforting.

Where am I? The question echoes in my mind, pulling me from the remnants of sleep.

I slowly crack open my eyes, and to my surprise, all I see is a vibrant burst of orange surrounding me. The walls are painted a warm, inviting shade that feels almost surreal, and soft, sheer curtains filter the sunlight, casting a gentle glow in the room.

Is this an orange room? I wonder, taking in the unusual decor that surrounds me, my heart racing with curiosity and confusion.

Wait!

I recently observed this room on the monitor in the security room; it's referred to as the passion room.

The color orange, a vibrant combination of red and yellow, symbolizes feelings of joy, excitement, and passion. The walls are painted a warm, buttery orange that radiates energy, while various artistic elements decorate the space, enhancing its lively atmosphere. It's designed to evoke a sense of enthusiasm and creativity, making it an ideal place for intimate gatherings that are both new and old.

As I immerse myself in the dimly lit atmosphere, my gaze drifts to the figure sprawled in the bed beside me.

It takes a moment for my eyes to adjust, and when they do, they are met with a cascade of fiery orange hair that frames a sultry, voluptuous body.

SHANNON!

Panic floods my mind.

Why can't I recall anything from last night?

Desperately, I reach over to the nightstand, where two glasses of water sit alongside a bottle of aspirin. I quickly swallow the pills, the bitter taste barely registers as I try to piece together the fragments of my memory.

Think, Corey!

What remnants of last night linger in the corners of my mind?

We indulged in the intoxicating Hearts of Chance and spun the bottle, and that's where my memories fade into a hazy blur.

Should I wake Shannon and see what fragments of the evening she holds onto?

I gently caress her shoulder, tracing my fingers softly along her skin, and trail kisses down her back. This intimate gesture feels achingly familiar and instinctively right.

She groans softly, "Ouch. Why does my head feel like it's been run over by a truck?"

"Tell me about it," I reply, rubbing my temples in an attempt to ease the pounding in my skull. "I think we definitely overindulged. What do you remember from last night? All I can recall is a blur of laughter, the thrill of playing spin the bottle, and the taste of the Hearts. But surely that can't explain why we woke up here, completely exposed and tangled in the sheets."

She finally turns to face me, her eyes sparkling with a mix of uncertainty and revelation. "Corey, I think I might remember some of what happened."

I lean in and plant a gentle kiss on her cheek, feeling the warmth radiate from her skin. "Go on, Spitfire. I believe we're beyond the point of keeping secrets from each other now."

A playful grin spreads across her face, a glimmer of mischief in her eyes. "You shared your past after we dove into something wild—something I never imagined I would do again."

"What did we do, Spitfire?" I ask, curiosity piquing in my tone.

She exhales softly, her expression growing serious. "We got married last night."

9

Kass

Once more, I find myself at Kastaways, that cherished haven nestled by the sea, which I've come to regard as my second home.

The salty breeze carries with it memories of laughter, tears, and the intricate tapestry of our lives woven together on these shores and in this club.

The plan I've devised is coming together seamlessly. With Corey and Shannon now officially married, a weight has lifted from my shoulders; the constant worry about her safety has vanished, replaced by a sense of relief.

In a rush of love and urgency, I commissioned a beautiful necklace for Shannon. I knew it would symbolize our connection while also serving a critical purpose—her safety. As I packed my bag, I carefully placed the intricately designed piece within, eager to present her with this token of support that carries so much meaning.

Hers is the same as the rest of us women who married into the Bratva—a glowing orange heart necklace that radiates warmth, love, and resilience. Yet hidden within its delicate design is a discreet tracker embedded securely to ensure her safety.

Each necklace is meticulously crafted, blending beauty with function, and Shannon's gleams with a vibrant hue that mirrors the passion and fire of her spirit. The trackers are ingeniously concealed within our jewelry, offering a layer of protection that is both effective and unobtrusive, allowing us to navigate our lives with a reassuring sense of security amid the chaos.

On a personal note, I am genuinely relieved that I decided to hand the reins over to Tori. Kastaways will always hold a special place in my heart, as it has been my passion and a significant part of my life for so long.

However, I've come to realize that I need to focus on repairing my marriage. The tension and strain we're experiencing are largely a result of my husband's choices, which have led to deep-seated issues between us. It truly pains me to reflect on the idea that I may not have been enough for him, and I often wonder if my own actions or shortcomings have contributed to the harm in our relationship. The weight of this realization is heavy, but I know that addressing these personal challenges is essential for moving forward.

As I enter Kastaways, my phone rings a number that doesn't call me much anymore, but I always love to talk to them.

The name on my screen reads "William Carter," illuminating the dimly lit room.

"Dad! How are you? How's Celeste? Are you up for a visit anytime soon?" I ask, a hint of eagerness in my voice. The thought of seeing him brings warmth to my heart, but I know he's been going through a tough time.

He lets out a long, weary sigh, a sound that immediately tightens the knot of concern in my stomach. "Hey, sweetheart. I'm doing okay, you know you can always drop in, but I realize you've got a lot on your plate. The reason I'm calling is about Celeste. I've heard some things and wanted to make sure you're aware of the situation."

I brace myself and suck in a deep breath, trying to steady my racing heart. "Okay, Dad. What's going on?"

His voice turns serious. "She divorced me a month ago. I should've filed first, to be honest. She cheated on me, and while she claims it was because I wasn't attentive enough to her needs, I won't go into the details—it's messy. But what concerns me is her plan, and you're part of it without her even realizing it."

"Dad, what the hell? I can't believe this! I will make her pay for this betrayal! Just say the word, and I'll handle it. No one disrespects my family and gets away with it! What could she possibly be trying to do that involves me?"

My blood boils at the thought of her treachery. How could she betray a man who poured so much into their relationship, who has always been unwaveringly loyal?

He sighs once more, this time a deeper, more exhausted sound. "She doesn't know you've created Kastaways. Apparently, she and her new boyfriend are planning to visit. He just got a membership at the club, and they're going to check it out together—see what she likes and what she can handle. Honestly, I'm indifferent to her choices, but I don't want her encroaching on your territory. I'd rather bring this to your attention than let Roman find out; he would definitely go on a warpath."

I sense the weight of his words, feeling an overwhelming surge of protectiveness toward him—and a fierce indignation toward her.

She plans to come to my club?

And she'll pay.

"Wow. Oh, don't worry, Dad, I can handle her if she dares to show her face. I'm actually in town, settled comfortably at the club. I'll swing by to visit you before I head back to Chicago. Should I call Massimo and ask him to deal with her?"

"NO! Umm, I mean no, sweetheart. You know he never liked her. Can you handle it on your own? I'm confident you will show some mercy."

Of course, Dad is apprehensive about unleashing the dark side of my husband.

"Okay, I'll take care of it. But if it gets out of hand, I won't hesitate to involve him. What's Celeste's boyfriend's name so I can keep an eye out?"

"Roy Boyce."

Well, this just got even more interesting.

No mercy will be shown.

"Alright, Dad, consider it done. I promise to be careful and merciful."

Little does Celeste know the storm she has just unleashed.

I am the Queen for a reason, and it's high time my reign is felt.

She betrayed the wrong family, aligning herself with an abuser—there can only be one fate for her.

Roy

Having a girlfriend in every state certainly comes with its advantages.

Celeste Carter, an intriguing woman I met during my travels, has agreed to spend some time with me at Kastaways today. She comes with a storied past.

Our arrangement has always been clear-cut: no strings attached, no commitments. It's a casual setup that suited both of us—until recently. We've been together for two years, but I was blindsided to discover that she was still legally married when we first started seeing each other.

My plan is to focus on having a good time while gathering as much information as possible about Tori and Connor. They should face the consequences of their actions, especially if they played a part in Cornelis' tragic death.

I won't let anyone stand in my way!

I am the forty-fifth richest person in New York, and I intend to use my resources and influence to uncover the truth.

I also wouldn't mind running into that charming little bartender again; she sparks a flame within me that I thought had long since extinguished. Her lively, expressive eyes captivate me in a way that draws me in, making me want to lose myself in them for hours on end. There's a warmth and mischief in her gaze that makes each interaction feel electric, reminding me how exhilarating it can be to connect with someone so effortlessly.

I always achieve my desires; no one, not even my girlfriend, can hold me back, and the law has no grip on my freedom.

Cornelis was the only person who ever truly understood me; he felt like a second father.

A father who molded me into a formidable force, a skilled operative, and a charming flirt. Thanks to him, I have become the most confident and charismatic version of myself.

I long for the warmth of my late wife's presence; her heart was vast and unconditional in its love.

She stood by me even through my moments of rage and cruelty, a testament to her unwavering spirit. I find myself craving another woman with that same resilience.

So far, Celeste has only seemed to respond to the tumult of our intimate battles, yet I can't help but wonder how she would react when the storm of my frustrations truly breaks.

Kass

I've meticulously crafted a thrilling plan; my husband, Massimo, is en route as we speak.

Our goal? To hunt and play within the seductive confines of the venue.

Celeste is about to experience an unforgettable evening—she utterly deserves everything that's about to unfold.

Massimo will rely on his irresistible charm to captivate her, drawing her away from her current companion, Roy. We have a special room—the passion room—reserved just for us, a hidden sanctuary no one else can access tonight.

Once Massimo has woven his spell, I'll make my dramatic entrance, adding an unexpected twist to the evening. Before that, we will set the stage for our performance, with me concealed behind an elegant mask. However, the spotlight will be on Massimo, allowing everyone to admire his handsome visage.

For those who frequent the club, Massimo's identity is no secret, but tonight they'll witness a side of him they've never seen before—his playful and seductive prowess on display.

I can hardly contain my excitement as I imagine the reactions of the crowd when they realize what's happening. Only Tori is in on the surprise of our act tonight, making it all the more exhilarating.

The thrill of the unknown mingling with my anticipation promises an unforgettable experience for all involved.

10

Shannon

I am married again!

Never did I envision finding myself on this path a second time, yet here I stand, embracing a beautiful new chapter of my life brimming with hope and excitement.

Corey and I recently celebrated our first day as a married couple, and I can genuinely say he is one of the sweetest souls I have ever had the pleasure to meet.

His kindness and sincere nature radiate in everything he does, from the way he listens with unwavering attention when I speak to the thoughtful little gestures that seem to flow from him effortlessly.

Although we chose not to share our first night together due to a prior commitment he needed to fulfill, I awoke this morning with an unexpected sense of happiness, a feeling that had eluded me for quite some time.

Stepping outside my front door, I was met with a breathtaking sight that took my breath away—a stunning bouquet of a dozen pristine white roses. Their delicate petals shimmered in the warm morning sunlight, each flower appearing to be kissed by golden rays, creating an enchanting display. This thoughtful gesture filled my heart with warmth and joy, reminding me of the beauty that can be found in the smallest acts of love.

The symbolism of white roses resonates profoundly with me, representing love, respect, loyalty, and friendship. I can genuinely envision a future filled with these values—and so much more—with Corey at my side. Every moment spent with him feels like a glorious celebration of these ideals, and I eagerly anticipate where this journey will lead us.

In comparison to my previous relationship, I truly believe that I will be alright.

Corey does not strike me as the type to be abusive. If he were, I am certain that Kass or Tori would have swiftly intervened.

This Bratva does not tolerate abuse of any kind.

As I make my way to Kastaways, I am filled with hope as to what the future holds for me and Corey.

As I reach to unlock Kastaways door, another dozen white roses sit on the steps this doesnt just have a tag that says "From Corey," there's a note.

The note reads,

I know we weren't planning on marrying each other, but the way your laughter dances in the air and the way your eyes sparkle when you talk about your passions fills me with hope for our future. I can't wait to explore the possibilities that lie ahead for us, Spitfire. The roses I picked for you symbolize my deep desire to love and cherish you, if you'll allow me the opportunity.

I hope we can sit down together and discuss our dreams and what we both truly want from this connection, because I am committed to being here for you, now and always. You deserve the world, and I want nothing more than to make that a reality for you.

With all my heart,

XOXO, Jump Drive

I can feel the warm, salty tears gently tracing pathways down my cheeks, a vivid testament to the intense emotions swirling tumultuously within me. In this poignant moment, I am wrapped in a cocoon of affection, feeling truly valued and cherished—an experience that eluded me during my tumultuous time with Roy.

It's as though a heavy burden has been lifted from my shoulders, granting me the freedom to embrace the exquisite beauty of being truly seen and appreciated for the person I am.

As I step into Kastaways, the inviting atmosphere envelops me, and I am greeted by the warm smiles of Tori and Kass, their familiar faces instantly putting me at ease, as if I've been wrapped in a comforting blanket.

"So you have an admirer, what does your husband think?" Tori teases with a playful glint in her eyes.

I smirk, feeling a rush of lightness. "He thinks that I deserve to be admired, and that admiration comes from him."

Now, casting a conspiratorial glance at my friends, I continue, "Now spill the beans! How on earth did you both let me tie the knot again?"

Tori shrugs nonchalantly, a mischievous smile creeping onto her lips. "Hear me out."

"What have you done?" I ask, my curiosity piqued.

Tori

A part of me feels like I've betrayed Shannon, a knot of guilt twisting in my stomach, but I refuse to go down alone in this mess.

"So it wasn't my idea," I say, trying to deflect the blame, "I was only following the Queen's orders." My voice trembles slightly, the weight of the truth pressing heavily on my chest.

Kass elbows me sharply in the side, her eyes wide with disbelief. "Really? Geez, way to throw me under the freight train!" Her annoyance is palpable, and I can tell she's furious that I'm shifting the responsibility onto her.

Shannon gasps, her expression a mix of shock and anger. "Kass! This was your idea? Why? Why marriage? Why me and Corey? You better have a good reason! And Tori, I know Kass is the Queen but you can say no, " Her voice rises, a hint of betrayal lacing her words as she searches Kass's face for an explanation. The tension in the air thickens, and I can feel the stakes rising as we navigate the storm of emotions swirling around us.

Kass placed a comforting hand on each of our shoulders, and the warmth of her touch calmed us instantly, a testament to her powerful presence as the reigning Queen.

"I needed you both safe," she began, her voice steady but filled with the urgency of the situation. "Corey is a strong protector; he will ensure you are secure. When I started snooping around and piecing together everything that was unfolding, I realized we couldn't take any chances. Something serious is about to go down, but please, let me finish explaining. When Tore called me, panicked and frantic because you were both in distress, I shifted into survival mode—a reflex that I have developed over time. I needed to protect you at all costs. Knowing how loyal and loving Corey can be, I made the decision to trust him with your safety. Yes, I orchestrated your marriage under the radar; I provided Tore with step-by-step instructions on how to make it happen without your knowledge. But I need all the important people in my life to be safe, and I stand by my actions without a single regret."

Well damn!

The Queen is not just a cold-hearted ruler; she's a whirlpool of emotions, fiercely protective of those she cares about.

I glanced over at Shan, feeling a surge of determination, "Yes, I was following orders, but my only aim was your happiness and safety."

Shan narrowed her eyes, the intensity of her gaze sending a shiver down my spine. "You have no idea what you both have just done."

Oh no!

What is Shan going to do?

"What did we do, Shan? How can we fix this?" My voice trembled slightly, uncertainty flooding my mind.

Kass sighed deeply, a mixture of irritation and understanding evident in her expression. "I know you're upset, but I'm not fixing a damn thing. Corey could easily erase your marriage in a heartbeat if he wanted to. But make no mistake, your safety will always be my top priority."

Shan's voice rose, brimming with indignation, "The consequence for both your reckless actions? You're stuck with me for life, because you both married me into the Bratva! Good fucking luck trying to shake off my stubborn ass!"

Suddenly, a fit of giggles erupted from Shan, her laughter echoing through the room like the sound of tinkling bells. "The worry on your faces was just so fucking worth it!"

"For heaven's sake, Shan! Don't do that!" I exclaimed, relief mixed with incredulity. "I thought you were genuinely pissed at us!"

With a soft smile, she replied, "Nah, you both know the hell I've been through before this. Compared to that, this is a cakewalk! I expect wedding presents from both of you, just so you know!"

At that moment, all felt right in the Kastaways' world, at least for now.

"I will get right on that, Shan," I assured her, a smile creeping onto my face as I began to relax.

Kass then reached into her purse and pulled out a small, elegantly wrapped box, its contents seemingly confirming what we all anticipated.

It was time for us to properly welcome Shannon into the Bratva, sealing our bond in a way that was both ceremonial and meaningful.

11

Shannon

Kass and Tori have officially welcomed me into the vibrant and eclectic fold of the Bratva, and now I find myself facing my first mission.

Tonight, Celeste, Kass's estranged stepmother, is coming to the club, and to make matters more complicated, she'll be accompanied by my ex-husband, Roy.

Do I care about their presence?

Not in the slightest!

Roy is just a chapter from my past, one that I've closed for good, while Cory represents everything that lies ahead for me; he's my future.

Kass has an exciting plan for the evening. The King and the Queen of the Bratva, renowned for their thrilling performances, are set to take center stage tonight.

Their shows are infamous around here, and I can only imagine the energy they'll bring to the room.

Having spent time at Kastaways, I've witnessed a myriad of wild and daring escapades unfold before my eyes. The atmosphere is electric, and I've become somewhat of a voyeur among the crowd, drawn into the allure of the unexpected.

While I find watching these encounters fascinating, I've barely had the chance to explore my own desires and sexuality.

Tonight, with the spotlight on the stage and the tension in the air, I can't help but wonder if that will finally change.

Though it's only been a few days, my husband is impressively wooing me with his unwavering affection. Each afternoon, he makes it a point to meet me at my house, eager to walk me to work. As he approaches, I can't help but smile at the sight of him, a bouquet of pristine white roses in hand.

Nestled in the center of the flowers is a striking single orange, its vibrant hue contrasting beautifully with the soft petals. The combination is not only a delightful surprise but also an endearing symbol of his creativity and thoughtfulness in expressing his commitment.

Could I truly love him?

Perhaps if we remain together and explore the possibilities of what this could become. Yet, I find myself wrestling with a multitude of fears, remnants of my experiences with Roy that I am struggling to cast aside.

Do I genuinely want Roy dead?

Absolutely not—if there's a way to avoid it.

Though he is far from a kind-hearted individual, I could never bring myself to wish death upon anyone. Such thoughts are too heavy, a burden I would rather not carry.

"Ready to play tonight, Spitfire?" Corey teased, a playful smirk dancing on his lips.

"Stop calling me that before I seriously consider spitting on you!" I shot back, half-laughing, half-annoyed.

"Ooh, are you into that sort of thing?" He raised an eyebrow, clearly enjoying my discomfort.

"Corey," I sighed, "you know I'm still figuring out what I'm into and what I actually like."

"Well, as we make the short walk to work, let's tackle some questions, and I'll help you uncover what you really want," he suggested, his arm casually sliding around my shoulder, warm and reassuring.

"I guess," I replied reluctantly, feeling a mix of curiosity and dread. "Just promise you won't laugh at my embarrassment."

"You know I'm bisexual, right?" Corey began, his tone shifting slightly more serious. "But I'm a committed bisexual. If I'm in a relationship, I'm all in for my partner, unless they express a desire to explore beyond our connection. How do you define your sexuality?"

I directed my gaze to the bustling sidewalk, watching the leaves fluttering down like confetti. "Honestly, I feel like I should say I'm straight, but there's something about women that I find undeniably attractive. I've just never had the chance to explore that side of myself. But between us, don't tell Tori, I wouldn't mind being with someone like her. If I were to connect with a woman, she would need to be kind and loving, but also tough as nails, because there's something incredibly attractive about strength." I paused, thinking carefully. "I know I'm a committed person as well, but with your openness, I really admire how honest you are about your own identity. I'm not sure how to define mine yet, but I have faith that I will get there. I trust you, Corey.

If you ever want to explore together, just let me know—I'm open to trying. After being sheltered for so long, maybe it could be a fun adventure."

It feels good to let that out and be able to be honest.

I slowly gaze up at him, his smile blinds me.

His arm tightens around my shoulder as he replies, "That was a weight lifted off of you wasn't it, baby? We can explore when you want to, no rush. I won't tell Tore. You know she would be flattered. Do you like things like spitting and licking?"

I feel my cheeks heat, "Spitting, I am not sure. Licking, yes! Every time I read about licking in a book, even if it's just sweet and not sexual, I instantly love it! What about you, Jump Drive?"

He smirks, a playful glint in his eyes, "Now she gets it right! I enjoy the thrill of spitting, but when it comes to licking, I completely agree—it can be so enticing. Would you let me lick you, baby?"

Oh my goodness! My face feels as hot and flushed as a ripe cherry tomato!

I clear my throat, desperately trying to suppress my embarrassment, "Maybe. But first, what's your favorite food?"

I need to steer this conversation away from anything too risqué and into safer territory.

He chuckles, a mischievous tone in his voice, "Women."

Good heavens!

"Corey! What do you mean by that?"

What just happened?

He pauses, his playful demeanor shifting as he leans in and teasingly licks my cheek, "Do you want me to show? I'm an expert when it comes to savoring the delicacies between women's legs. I may be bi, but trust me, I love to indulge."

Oh my!

I was attempting to change the subject, only for him to turn it right back!

"I've never experienced that, so I wouldn't really know," I admit, my heart racing.

He whispers in my ear as we approach Kastaways, "Hmm, then be ready tonight when we're set to play. I want to show you just how good it can be. Kass wants us to have our fun while she and Massimo are performing on stage tonight.

They've arranged for the bar to shut down so that all the employees can fully indulge alongside us."

A wave of warmth colors my cheeks as I try to hide my embarrassment. "Are we actually going to watch Kass and Massimo? I've never seen anyone have sex before, but just the thought of it sends a thrill through me."

"It's called voyeurism, darling. But it's entirely up to you. If you're interested, I could reserve us a private cubicle."

I look up at him, my heart racing, "I'd really like that. Could we sit in the second row to make sure we have the best view?"

He presses a gentle kiss to my cheek and holds the door to Kastaways open for me, a playful smile dancing on his lips. "Your wish is my command!"

Well, this just got interesting! I hope he has a ravenous appetite for what's to come!

Roy

Tonight is the night I've been waiting for—Celeste and I are finally going to have some fun together. After a long period fixated on my plans for revenge, I've decided it's time to take a break and unwind.

Kastaways, the trendy club downtown, has been buzzing with excitement lately and is advertising a big performance on the main stage. Celeste casually mentioned how much she wanted to see the show, and I figured I could indulge her just this once.

I'm fully aware of the dynamic between us; she knows I'm not seeking anything serious, and I've come to terms with the fact that she has three boyfriends. It's all part of our arrangement—no strings attached, just good times.

One thing I always prioritize is ensuring her safety; I never take chances when it comes to our intimacy. We've established a solid rule: we always, without exception, use protection. Tonight, as I prepare for our evening together, I'm filled with anticipation. I look forward to letting go of the usual weight of my anxieties and simply embracing the joy of being in her presence.

I can't wait to see that fiery spark in that pretty little bartender, that vibrant energy that draws me in. Maybe I'll even have the chance to tease and play with her mischievously.

Those captivating eyes pull me in every time, like a deep ocean I want to dive into. They make me forget about everything else, urging me to surrender to the moment and completely lose myself in the connection we share, well, the connection I have.

But I am sure I can convince her to like me, I can be a prince for her.

12

Corey

Shannon is gently stealing my icy heart, melting its chill with the radiant warmth of her vibrant spirit. Each smile she shares feels like the first golden rays of sunlight breaking through after a long, bitter winter, igniting a sense of hope and renewal within me.

These past two weeks with Shannon have been nothing short of extraordinary, filling my days with joyous laughter, cherished companionship, and an earnest desire to see her happiness blossom. Her presence feels like a sweet melody, weaving itself into the very fabric of my life, leaving me yearning for more of her infectious joy.

Recently, I confided in my dear friend Tori about my longing to find the perfect ring for Shannon—an emblem that captures her essence and showcases the depth of commitment we have. Together, we embarked on an inspiring creative journey, sketching designs and selecting gemstones that reflect her vibrant personality and unique beauty.

I envisioned a piece that wouldn't just symbolize our budding relationship, but would also be a testament to her individuality. It has become a tradition between the Bravita men to give their women a handcrafted ring to show how much they mean to them. Even though my feelings are still growing for Shannon, I want to continue this tradition and show her that she is my flower.

As we sifted through options, a whirlwind of ideas filled the room, and I could sense the thrill of possibility electrifying the air between us. Shannon is like a radiant flower in my life; she infuses every moment with vivid color and joy, coaxing my heart and soul into full bloom with her infectious laughter and gentle spirit.

I find myself thinking of her as my rose—a stunning blossom that, while occasionally thorny due to the shadows of her past, never truly pierces me. Instead, those thorns serve as a reminder of her resilience and strength, making our connection even more profound. I can feel the spark between us igniting, a flame of passion and understanding that grows brighter with each shared glance and whispered word.

Shannon

Tonight's the night I'm eagerly anticipating, as Corey is excited to watch the show and perhaps take our intimacy to the next level.

Honestly, I don't have a vivid memory of our first encounter just two weeks ago; we both indulged a bit too much in drinks, and it feels like a blur.

To prepare for tonight, I've gone all out. I made a special trip to the spa that Kass and Tori recommended, where I treated myself to a full-body pampering session.

I underwent a thorough waxing, leaving my skin feeling smooth and soft to the touch. My hair also got a makeover; I had my orange ends brightened to make sure they really pop and draw attention.

As a final touch, I splurged on a pedicure, opting for a vibrant bright orange color on my toes, which now look stunning. I even decided to get orange acrylic nails that perfectly match.

Overall, I feel incredibly confident and empowered. It's as if I'm blossoming like a flower, fully revealing my beauty and femininity in this moment!

Kass and Massimo have an intriguing scene planned, shrouded in mystery and allure. The only details they've shared hint at a captivating performance that promises to enthrall the audience. Kass will don a beautifully crafted mask, intricately designed to conceal her identity while simultaneously accentuating her allure. This enigmatic performance places her in a vulnerable position, at the mercy of Massimo, whose commanding presence is sure to heighten the tension and anticipation surrounding their encounter.

As I think about this unfolding drama, I can't help but feel that it will stir something deep within me—awakening desires I didn't realize were dormant.

My past has left me feeling sheltered and guarded, particularly after enduring an abusive relationship with Roy that stifled my spirit. But now, life—or perhaps Kass—seems to have a plan for me that is luxuriously sweet and full of promise.

For the first time, I truly feel protected and valued. It's as if I've finally stepped into the light, desired by someone who embraces the real me instead of trying to reshape me into what they want.

Corey, with his regal demeanor and kind heart, is a king deserving of a queen. I find myself wondering if I can embody not only that role but also something even more profound—someone who stands beside him as a partner and equal.

What secrets lie in store for Kass and Massimo in this performance? The anticipation is palpable, and I'm eager to discover the depth of their artistry and the complexities of desire they will unveil on stage.

Kass

As I slide my curvy figure into the eye-catching, bright red lingerie my husband gifted me, a wave of nervous energy washes over me, making my heart race.

Massimo, always in tune with my instincts, insisted we forgo any rehearsal for our upcoming routine. He desires my reactions to unfold spontaneously, raw and unfiltered.

I'm acutely aware of how my body responds to his every touch; it's instinctual, electric. Conversely, I know how he reacts when another man brushes against me, an irritable protector ready to spring into action.

He would do anything to protect me, including eliminating anyone who dares to tread on our sacred bond — unless, of course, it's someone he trusts.

That's why he chose Connor to participate in our scene. Tori, our mutual confidant and friend, specifically instructed Massimo that Connor is off-limits when it comes to harm. I can feel the weight of that decision, both a comfort and a source of tension.

Trust, however, runs both ways: Massimo trusts Connor, and I trust Tori completely.

Tori has given me a few tantalizing tips on how to ignite Connor's interest, but the butterflies in my stomach flutter in a chaotic dance.

Massimo is my king, my heart — yet today marks a pivotal moment in our relationship. He's allowing us to explore the boundaries of our love, to see if inviting another person into our lives can work.

However, there's a dark shadow looming over this night. Massimo has no idea that I possess knowledge he's kept hidden — the truth about his indiscretions during our two years apart while I poured my heart and soul into building Kastaways.

The club's name echoes my pain; it reflects how he cast aside my feelings. He chose to push me away to indulge the whims of another woman.

She deceived him with a web of lies, claiming to be single and searching for love, while in reality, she was married, a mother of two, seeking a fleeting escape in the arms of a wealthy sugar daddy.

The irony stings — she showed him the depths of betrayal, but that betrayal is not the cruellest twist. Someone else directed her towards his naïve heart, and that very person is set to arrive at Kastaways tonight.

What she doesn't realize is that I possess an arsenal of truths. She has entangled herself in a web she can't escape, and soon she will learn what it means to incur the Queen's wrath, especially when threatening the sanctity of the queen's family and her loyal subjects.

She should pray for my king's restraint; my emotions are a tempest, and the heft of my favorite knife rests in my purse.

My reign, forged in love and tempered by betrayal, will never die.

Corey

I need tonight to be absolutely perfect; Shannon deserves a magical evening to unwind and truly let go of her worries.

Our connection has been deepening in ways I never anticipated; she's slowly but surely opening up to me, sharing her dreams and fears that she once kept locked away.

I'm becoming her safe haven, her comfort zone, and it feels as if I'm on top of the world, buoyed by the trust and warmth she extends to me.

To me, she's like a rose, vibrant and full of life, blossoming beautifully right before my eyes.

As she sheds her thorns, the remnants of past hardships, her petals unfurl gracefully, radiating with an exquisite beauty that captivates everyone around her. Tonight, I want to celebrate just how stunning she is, both inside and out.

I know how nervous she is, especially given how both of us struggle to remember the exact moment when our intimacy first began to blossom. It feels like a blurred memory, lost in the haze of that wild night at the bar, the dim lights casting playful shadows and laughter echoing above the clinking of glasses.

If only we hadn't gotten so carried away with the shots and the music, the way it pulsed through us, urging us to let go of our inhibitions. I can still picture her smile, bright and carefree, as we danced with abandon, the world around us fading into the background.

But now, all that remains are fragments of that evening, slipping through our fingers like sand, leaving us both yearning to grasp the magic that transformed our wild night into a wild but sweet marriage.

I've secured our cozy cubicle for tonight, and we're lucky enough to have the most breathtaking view of the stage.

It's essential for her to feel the warmth of intimate passion, where every touch and glance reverberates with mutual desire, rather than endure the harshness of partners who take what they want without considering her feelings or aspirations. She deserves to experience a tender connection that honors her emotional and physical needs, fostering an environment where she can truly embrace every moment.

She needs the freedom to explore and express everything she yearns for and desires in her sexuality, unreservedly embracing her fantasies and preferences.

This journey of self-discovery should be met with respect and attentiveness, allowing her to seek pleasure that is fulfilling and meaningful, and to engage in experiences that resonate deeply with her inner self.

Kass said she bought Shannon a new outfit to make her feel beautiful tonight.

I can't wait to see how radiant she looks.

Shannon

"Shut up and put this on! I will not take no for an answer! You're going to look stunning!"

My head hangs low as I gaze at the outfit Kass just thrust into my hands.

At least it's not short; it's a flowing, vibrant orange dress that sweeps the ground, its long length punctuated by daring splits on either side, revealing glimpses of my legs that end just before the hip.

Oh goodness, with my chest size, I can already imagine how the curves will spill out of the low-cut neckline, where only delicate strings provide the slightest semblance of coverage.

"Kass, you can pull this off, not me. I know that I am only a little bit bigger than you, but you have so much more confidence than I do," I confess, my voice tinged with self-doubt.

Kass gasps, her eyes widening in disbelief. "Do not ever talk about yourself like that! After everything you went through, you are a total hottie! Your body is beautiful, and I know it's taking time for you to embrace it, but that man looks at you like you are a blazing fire that he wants to let consume him! He has flames dancing in his eyes every time he glances your way. I know you're feeling nervous, but tonight is about revenge for me and intimacy for you. Let that man ignite your world!"

I slowly lift my gaze to meet Kass's, a mixture of determination and uncertainty swirling within me. "Fine! Should I be daring and wear no underwear, or stick with my sweet and innocent look? You really know how to boost a woman's confidence," I say, a smile creeping onto my lips.

Kass bursts into laughter, her infectious energy filling the room. "This is a kink club, so my vote is to shock the hell out of Corey by going commando! Shan, you have this natural aura of sweet and innocent, but it's time to let yourself breathe and explore everything you want to be! That man would burn down the world for you; the least you can do is allow him to set your body on fire."

She's absolutely right, and the realization sparks a fire within me.

But I can't resist teasing her, just like everyone else does. I sweep into a mock bow, a playful smirk on my face. "Yes, my Queen, your word is law."

She playfully smacks my shoulder, her laughter filling the air. "Damn right! Now go change and own the night!"

I nod, determination flooding my veins. Tonight, I will shed the petrified wallflower identity that has haunted me for too long and let the wild rose within me finally bloom.

Corey

The performance is set to commence in just ten minutes, and the anticipation in the air is palpable. As I scan the crowded room for Shannon, my heart sinks—she is nowhere to be found. Just a moment ago, I caught sight of Kass, leaning casually against the wall with a mischievous glint in her eye.

With a cryptic smirk playing on her lips, she leaned closer and said, "Let Shan burn with you."

The words hung heavily in the air, their meaning elusive and frustratingly unclear. What could she possibly mean by that?

My name is not Arson, yet I can't shake the feeling that I'm missing some hidden context. I know that Arson is always at the center of excitement and intrigue, while I seem stuck on the sidelines, grappling with computers instead of reveling in the fun.

I reach our cubicle and wait for Shannon. As I step inside, I see the plate of chocolate that Kass left.

She told us the other day she would be leaving us a sweet treat to use to "sweeten" our intimacy.

I sense Shan's presence before I even catch a glimpse of her.

An overwhelming wave of hope and comfort washes over me, wrapping around my heart like a warm embrace.

As I turn to face her, my pulse quickens, igniting a fervent fire within me!

The flames of desire flare to life!

Her orange dress clings to her voluptuous curves, cascading around her like flickering flames, and I find myself captivated, unable to look away.

The words spill from my lips in a rush, a blend of admiration and spontaneity, "You're absolutely radiant; you could set me ablaze!"

A fiery glint ignites in her eyes, transforming her gaze into a playful challenge as she replies, "Careful what you wish for, Jump Drive."

In that fleeting moment, her flirtation hangs in the air between us like a delicate thread, and my heart takes flight, soaring with the exhilarating thrill of possibility. The warmth of her presence envelops me, each playful glance igniting a spark of hope and anticipation.

"I know exactly what I want your nickname to be, baby," I say, my voice low and teasing, inviting her curiosity. "Do you want to hear it?"

The fire in her eyes dances with mischief, a playful challenge reflected in her smile. "Baby is already cute enough," she replies, a teasing lilt in her voice.

"Cute doesn't do you justice, though," I counter, my gaze locking onto hers, intense and sincere. "You are shining bright and blooming, like a rose unfurling its petals to the sun. Your thorns are slowly falling away, revealing the beauty underneath. So for me, you're not just a baby; you are my Rose. Some days, you will be pure and white, radiating innocence, and other days, you'll burst forth in vibrant shades of orange, exuding warmth and allure. But no matter what color you choose to portray, I will always be here by your side, unwavering and devoted."

The club lights dim, signaling the performance starting.

My Rose playfully nudges me onto the couch, her eyes sparkling with mischief. "Let's watch the show," she says, her voice teasing, "who knows what will happen tonight, Firecracker?"

But honestly, I won't be paying attention to the stage.

All my focus is on her—a vibrant presence that ignites my very soul. She's setting me ablaze with her laughter and warmth!

13

Roy

I felt a mix of excitement and curiosity as I anticipated the evening ahead. Celeste had been raving about the shows ever since I paid the membership fee, sharing stories of thrilling performances and captivating atmospheres from everyone she had talked to.

I've always found the allure of watching people engage in intimate acts and explore their kinks fascinating, so when she proposed going to the event, I quickly reserved us a spot.

As I sat in front of my computer, ready to finalize the $250 payment for our place, the screen unexpectedly flipped to a confirmation message before I even entered my card information.

A sense of disbelief washed over me. To ease my mind, I decided to call the club directly, just to verify that our names were indeed on the guest list for what promised to be an unforgettable night.

This club, known for its reputation, is always impeccably clean, despite the nature of its activities as a sex club. The cubicles, designed for both comfort and anonymity, are perfectly aligned and stocked with everything one might need to enjoy the performances and watch other couples indulge in their desires.

The atmosphere here is liberating, allowing individuals with a diverse range of kinks to explore their fantasies without judgment. It creates a sanctuary where everyone's preferences are respected. However, I find myself grappling with a darker urge, one that is frowned upon in this space—my longing for the thrill of beating without consent. The cries and screams that echo in my mind ignite a passion within me, but I remind myself to exercise restraint in this public setting.

One of the reasons I feel a deep void is because of Tara. She understood me in ways that others couldn't; she was willing to embrace my more extreme inclinations and experienced ecstasy in pain as I showed her the love I desperately needed.

As Celeste and I settle into our cubicle, I can't help but steal glances at the couple in front of us. The woman has striking features, her eyes carrying a seductive allure that draws me in. With a magnetic charisma, she has an almost hypnotic presence—a perfect blend of beauty and confidence that leaves me yearning to be lost in her gaze, to explore the depths of her body and desires.

As she turns her head, revealing her identity, I see it's Shannon—the charming bartender I met during my first visit here. Her warm smile brightens the dimly lit bar, and I can't help but admire her. She has an incredible figure, with curves that catch the eye and a confident grace in the way she carries herself.

It's hard to ignore the thought of how lovely it would be to share more than just a casual conversation with her, or maybe share a bet.

Or would she let me beat her with my belt?

14

Shannon

Kass is really a fucking Queen, excuse my language, but I am so damn impressed!

She stepped onto the stage, radiating confidence in a striking, sheer one-piece lace body suit that glimmered a vivid red under the spotlight. The fabric clung to her curves, accentuating her figure, while a black and red tiara sat delicately atop her head, glistening mischievously.

The audience fell silent, captivated by the spectacle unfolding before them.

With a fierce gaze locked onto Massimo, the head of the Bratva, she smirked. "You see the crown on his head?" She gestured toward him, her voice dripping with sarcasm. "He can keep it."

In one fluid motion, she snatched her own crown from her head, the tiara's jewels catching the light, and tossed it into Massimo's lap, where he sat bound to a chair, his expression a mix of rage and disbelief.

"He can reign all he wants," she continued, her tone filled with defiance, "but I will reign with revenge! My dear husband despises it when other men touch me, yet he allows other women to touch him." Her eyes sparkled with mischief. "So now, he must watch my pleasure rise at the hands of another man." She paused, letting her words sink in. "Cheating is never okay, especially in our world. He will learn that what his Queen says is law. I hope everyone enjoys the show; I know I will."

Just then, Connor emerged from the shadows and stepped onto the stage with an air of charm. He blew a playful kiss to his wife, who returned the gesture with a confident wink, unfazed by the chaos unfolding.

The intricate dynamics of couples in the Bratva world never ceased to amaze me—the fierce loyalty, unwavering trust, and deep commitment they shared were intoxicatingly powerful, transforming what could have been mere chaos into something undeniably thrilling.

I turn to Corey, "I wish I had her body and confidence."

"No, my Rose. You're the perfect bouquet. Never dim your brightness. You are everything and more to me. How is the show making you feel?"

I glance back at the stage, and Massimo has tears in his eyes; he knows he messed up.

The tears flow as Connor eats Kass out; her one-piece is crotchless. Kass knew exactly what she was doing.

I can't seem to tear my gaze away from Kass and Connor; their chemistry is electric and it's igniting something within me, a sensation that travels like a warm current through my body.

"It draws me in, making me crave to witness more and more of their connection. But it's not just that—I feel an urge to experience something wild, something different," I admit, a hint of excitement bubbling in my voice.

Corey blinks at me, momentarily surprised. "What exactly do you want to try?" he asks, curiosity piqued.

I lean in closer, the electric tension in the air making my heartbeat quicken. "I want to set your world on fire," I whisper, a playful glint of mischief dancing in my eyes.

"My heart already burns for you, Rose. What more can I give you?" he replies, his voice thick with desire.

Feeling a rush of confidence, I rise from the couch and sink to my knees before him. With deliberate care, I undo Corey's belt, the soft rustle of fabric breaking the charged silence. I remove his pants and underwear, discarding them casually onto the couch, a bold declaration of intent.

I then stand tall but lean down just enough so that my curves align perfectly with his gaze, drawing him in.

"You can sit back, relax, and let the thrill wash over you," I tease, my voice a sultry invitation that dances in the heated air, thick with electric anticipation.

"What do you need, Rose?" he asks, his eyes sharp with curiosity.

I rest my hands lightly on his shoulders, feeling the warmth radiating from him, and I can sense the eagerness pulsing beneath his skin.

I straddle him perfectly, and he slides right into my entrance.

I moan, "Fuck me, baby! You have me burning up!"

That's all the encouragement he needs.

"No panties, fuck! You're just as diabolical as Kass. Tell me what you want, Rose! How do you want it? This is all about you, let me take care of you."

I lick his neck and jerk my hips in a circular motion, "I want you to fuck me like I am the only one that matters!"

"Always, Rose, always."

I don't have a chance to catch my breath, he grips my hips for dear life, and thrusts his hips forward.

"Can I take you hard and fast, Rose? I need you right now, I swear I will make it up to you!"

I smile and kiss his lips, "No need, baby. Take me, hard and rough! I want everything you will give me."

"Bloom, my flower! Take it all!"

Oh, I will take it all!

I can't stifle my moans.

"Baby! Yes! Corey!"

He kisses me, caresses my back, and makes me feel safe while setting my body on fire.

His pace is fast and rough and pure ecstasy and passion.

"Take it, baby, come on my dick. GIVE IT ALL TO ME!"

Yes!

I love it when he raises his voice; it doesn't scare me, it excites me.

He makes me feel like I really am the only thing that matters to him, the difference between and Roy is night and day.

After ten minutes of pure bliss my orgasm subsides.

He kisses my neck, "Was that enough for you, my Rose?"

I bite his neck and he moans and grabs my ass.

"That was pure fire," I exclaimed, still buzzing from the exhilarating moment we just shared. "Can we do it again?"

He chuckled softly, a warm smile spreading across his face, his eyes sparkling with mischief. "Anytime you want. Just say the word."

In that instant, I felt a rush of euphoria wash over me. It was as if the world around us melted away, leaving just the two of us suspended in a bubble of joy.

High on life.

High on bliss.

Each shared touch sparked an electric connection, while every lingering glance wove a thread of intimacy between us, drawing our hearts ever nearer.

I think I might be falling in lust, caught in a fierce whirlwind of desire that ignites every part of me. The thrill is intoxicating, pulling me closer to a fire pit of passion that I willingly dive into, heart racing and senses alive. Strangely, I don't crave rescue; the flames are enticing, illuminating shadows of my past that I'm eager to leave behind.

Could this be the moment where I finally shed the weight of yesterday? Am I truly on the brink of embracing something new, something bold?

Is it possible that I'm not just flirting with lust, but instead, I'm teetering on the edge of falling in love?

Roy

I can't focus on Celeste, her soft skin brushing against mine, as my eyes remain fixed on Shannon and her partner, lost in their performance. The room is filled with a mix of low music and hushed whispers, creating an intimate atmosphere that heightens my senses. Celeste, oblivious to my distraction, is more captivated by the movements of the two men on stage, their bodies exuding passion and strength.

I can feel the warmth radiating from Celeste beside me, but my mind is completely absorbed in my own private show. The way Shannon laughs playfully, her eyes sparkling as she engages with her partner, pulls me deeper into the moment. It's a scene filled with passion and energy that draws me in, making me forget about everything else around us.

Shannon is asserting her dominance over her partner's body, compelling him to fulfill her desires with an intensity that is undeniably thrilling. The sensation is undeniably captivating, but it doesn't quite resonate as my ultimate preference. I yearn for the power to guide the experience myself, to be in charge and explore the depths of pleasure on my own terms.

Their passion is evident, the sweet nothings they are whispering to each other is nauseating.

"Baby!"

Her moan sounds so familiar.

"Fuck me, baby! You have me burning up!"
That voice—an intoxicating melody that sends my heart racing and my pulse quickening. But why is it affecting me so deeply?

"Baby! Yes! Corey!"

The way she breathes out the word "baby" sends jolts through me, each syllable a spark igniting a fire in my chest.

Her voice, filled with warmth and familiarity, echoes in my mind like a long-lost song. It sounds strikingly like my Tara—the love I thought I had lost forever.

But that can't be possible!

I had the police confirm it countless times, the grim reality etched into my memory: they told me she was gone, that the body they found was indeed hers, unmistakably hers!

Celeste has finally left me alone and has dragged some man to one of the playrooms.

I cautiously step to the edge of my small cubicle, the fabric dividers offering only minimal privacy, desperate for a clearer view of Shannon as she sits at her desk.

What the hell?!

Right there, displayed prominently on her thigh, is undeniable evidence of the betrayal. A vivid scar, intricately designed, catches the light and pulls my attention like a magnet.

A deep, jagged "X" is carved into her right thigh, a stark reminder of that day. It was the day she decided to wear a skirt that was far too short, strutting through the grocery store as if she didn't have a care in the world. The way she flaunted herself, drawing the attention of other men, ignited a fierce anger within me.

As I trace the scar with my fingertips, a shiver runs through me. I can feel the heat of that anger swelling in my veins, a relentless fire I cannot extinguish. I whisper under my breath, words laced with a chilling determination, "I am coming for you, Tara!"

You are my wife—bound to me in ways you might not fully understand. No matter how far you think you can run, you cannot escape the reality of what we share.

The ties that bind us are strong, and I will always find you.

15

Shannon

As I gaze into Corey's eyes, my heart flutters with a mix of excitement and nerves.

Still straddling him, I nestle my head against his shoulder, the familiar scent of his cologne grounding me even as my mind races.

I take a deep breath and whisper, "I can't shake this feeling that someone is watching us. I know it's not uncommon in this area, but could you look around and see if anyone seems to be observing us? My anxiety is peaking right now."

His arms tighten protectively around me, providing a sense of security. "Don't apologize, my Rose," he murmurs softly, his voice steady and reassuring. "I'm checking for you."

I appreciate his understanding in this moment of vulnerability. "Thank you," I reply, squeezing his hand as a silent way of asking for reassurance.

He scans the dimly lit room, shadows dancing across the walls, his brow furrowing in concern as he takes in our secluded surroundings. "No one is watching us, Rose. Are you okay? Did I hurt you in any way? What can I do to make you feel better?" His voice trembles slightly, a warm tremor that radiates genuine concern, cutting through the anxiety swirling inside me.

I lift my gaze, meeting his stunning, deep-set eyes, and the depth of compassion reflected there brings a wave of comfort. It's as if I can almost feel the warmth of his affection wrapping around me like a soft blanket.

Driven by an overwhelming surge of emotion, I press my lips against his roughly, pouring my feelings into that single kiss, devouring the moment as if it might make all my worries vanish.

"Nothing, unless you're willing to go get ice cream with me," I say, my voice slightly breathless. "It's always been my favorite thing to do after sex—sharing a sweet treat with my partner. My last boyfriend didn't appreciate that, though. He always made comments about how fat I am, and it made me self-conscious. So, I completely understand if you feel the same way and prefer not to indulge."

As the words escape my lips, I brace myself for his reaction, my heart fluttering with equal parts anxiety and hope. I long for him to see beyond the scars of my past, to embrace the simple joy of enjoying something sweet together, as I feel the weight of doubt pressing down on me.

He cups my face gently but firmly, his warm hands anchoring me in the moment. "Get those negative thoughts out of your head right now!" he declares, his voice resonating with conviction. "You're a beautiful flower, nothing can make you wilt!" His intensity melts away my insecurity, and I find solace in his unwavering gaze. "Fuck him! He treated you like you were a thorn in his side, but that is not what you are to me. You're the star of my garden—the radiant blossom that lights up even the gloomiest of days."

Feeling a rush of warmth fill my cheeks, I can't help but smile as he continues, "You want ice cream? Then that's what my Rose will get! Never hesitate to ask for what you want, my love," he insists, a fierce determination in his voice. "I would burn down the world for you if that's what it takes. I would make the sky rain ash if that is your wish. Shed your past because I am your future, and I am not going anywhere. We are married until one of us dies for real—not just because Kass decides it's time to disappear."

His words wrap around me like a protective embrace, each declaration igniting a spark of confidence within. "So answer me this: cherry, mint, or brownie?" he asks, his eyes sparkling with mischief.

I blush, the warmth spreading through me, buoyed by his faith in me. His unwavering support lifts my spirits higher than I thought possible.

I lean in, pressing a soft kiss to his cheek, and whisper with a teasing smile, "All three."

He tilts his head, his lips grazing my skin as he licks my neck playfully, his voice low and sultry. "I can't wait to lick all of it off of you." The thrill of his words sends shivers down my spine, making me feel desired and cherished all at once.

Corey

I will give my Rose the world! Everything she deserves and more.

Roy deserves to pay dearly for the pain he inflicted on Shannon, a wound that runs deeper than he could ever understand.

His gaze pierced through the crowded room, locking onto us with an intensity that made my skin crawl and my heart race. Each second felt like an eternity, as the weight of his stare hung heavy in the air.

Anxiety bubbled within Shannon; she could feel the unsettling pressure of someone's gaze boring into her, though she remained blissfully unaware that it belonged to that despicable man who had tormented her.

I am determined to delve deep into Roy's past; if he isn't careful, I will uncover secrets that could leave him reeling. He might not make it out of Mississippi unscathed, and I will make sure of that.

He had no right, absolutely no right, to abuse her in any form, and the sheer audacity he displayed by calling her fat is beyond comprehension!

Before her reconstructive surgery, Shannon weighed a mere 180 pounds—a number that, in reality, was perfectly healthy for her height and build. So what if she tips the scales at 200 pounds now? It only reflects the stronger, more confident woman she has become.

She is not unhealthy; in fact, she leads an active lifestyle filled with yoga classes and weekend hikes, a testament to her commitment to fitness and well-being. For Roy to have instilled in her the belief that she was overweight at 180 pounds is nothing short of madness. It's a manipulation that gnaws at my heart.

He clearly has no appreciation for genuine feminine beauty, mistaking size for worth, and that is a tragedy that must be addressed!

Who is the enigmatic woman he brought along with him?

What tales lie beneath her surface?

The intensity of Kass's gaze as she listened to the woman's speech at the beginning of the performance was palpable; something felt amiss.

Kass is not one to harbor hatred; she possesses a remark-able ability to uncover the good in everyone she encounters.

Yet the unmistakable disdain etched across her face and the tension in her posture told a different story.

It seemed clear that neither of them was prepared for the tumultuous arena they had just stepped into.

I won't rush to conclusions until I've conducted thorough checks on both, but one thing is certain—they will not tarnish my Rose.

16

Tori

The performance last night was nothing short of electrifying!

Kass finally got her well-deserved revenge, a scenario that Massimo surprisingly consented to. You could almost feel the tension in the air as he watched Connor push Kass to her absolute breaking point, a mix of agony and thrill playing across his face.

My husband was irresistibly hot and exuded a sexy confidence that made my heart race, igniting an urge to leap into his arms right then and there!

I've never shied away from sharing, and it's hard to imagine Connor and I finding another partner who complements our dynamic as perfectly as Spence did.

Yet, we grapple with the painful reality every single day—that he is gone, never to return to us.

Despite the heartache, we are committed to raising our baby with all the love from both of his dads. We are overjoyed that the paternity test has confirmed Spence as the biological father. It brings us solace, knowing that a part of Spence will always remain with us, forever woven into our family.

Kass has meticulously devised a plan to eliminate the thorn that is Celeste from her life.

To lure her in, we've crafted a tantalizing invitation specifically for Celeste, enticing her to experience an exclusive VIP dungeon at Kastaways—a place shrouded in mystery and dark allure.

It baffles me that she hasn't yet recognized Kass. After all, if someone were married to a person with children, one would expect a certain level of familiarity.

Kass reviewed the video footage from the performance, captivated by the sight of Celeste, blissfully engrossed, utterly unaware that her enjoyment was taking place right alongside the very woman she had wronged.

My role in Kass's grand scheme is singular but crucial: I must secure Celeste in the dungeon. After that, Kass will take charge and orchestrate the rest of the plan.

The Queen is not one to shy away from protecting her family. In this case, Celeste has crossed a line by meddling with the two people most dear to Kass: her husband and her father.

Celeste better brace herself for the storm ahead and plead for mercy, for the consequences of her actions will be severe.

17

Kass

K astaways is closed to the public for an entire week, shrouded in an air of secrecy.

I have a carefully planned revenge to execute, but for now, I'll set that aside.

Right now, I'm going to indulge in some time with my husband, who is desperate to atone and make amends for his past transgressions.

But deep down, what do I truly desire?

I want him to confront the truth—that he has wronged me in ways too deep to ignore.

Watching Connor care for me became a form of poetic justice, a mirrored punishment for my husband's mistakes.

He loathes the idea of other men touching me; thus, it feels only fitting for him to witness the intimate attention I receive from another man.

As I stroll through the dimly lit club, the heavy silence envelops me, pulling me deeper into my thoughts.

Memories swirl like the colorful, pulsating lights that dance around the room, each flicker reminding me of the heartfelt purpose behind this establishment's creation.

This place was envisioned as a sanctuary—an inviting refuge for individuals from all walks of life, whether they were weary workers craving a moment of respite after long hours or friends jubilantly celebrating life's milestones. It serves as a haven where people can unwind, connect over shared experiences, and feel secure in a world that often feels chaotic and unpredictable.

The soft hum of animated conversations, the clinking of glasses filled with vibrant cocktails, and the rhythmic beats of music interweaving in the background create an atmosphere that fosters vulnerability and genuine connection, making it a truly exceptional gathering place for everyone lucky enough to step inside.

But beneath the glittering façade of laughter and light, I unearthed a harsh and painful reality. While I poured my heart and soul into building this oasis of joy, my husband, Massimo, was busy indulging in secret affairs with other women, seduced not just by opportunity but by the manipulative plans of my stepmother, Celeste. She had woman after woman lined up to seduce my husband, and she was paying them to do so with my father's money.

The betrayal cuts deep; it feels like a dagger aimed directly at the core of my family, twisting slowly with each revelation I uncover.

Celeste won't get away with this. Not only did she attempt to shatter my marriage, but she also inflicted irreparable damage to my father's heart, a heart that had already weathered so much. His love for her was profound and sincere, full of trust and devotion, and yet she devastated him by repeatedly cheating throughout their years together.

This morning, when I visited Dad at his modest home, his voice was laced with sorrow, yet tinged with an unexpected relief. He confided in me that he felt fortunate I had insisted on a prenuptial agreement before marrying Celeste. Because of that, she will walk away with nothing due to her own infidelity, her actions now carry real consequences, and fortunately, my father has the evidence to back it up, including messages and photos that forever tarnish the image she once held.

As if ensnared in a twisted fairy tale, Corey, my steadfast friend and unwavering confidant, has taken it upon himself to keep a watchful eye on Celeste. He's provided me with a treasure trove of sordid details about her secret escapades, ensuring that I remain fully apprised of her every move. With this knowledge coursing through me, I feel a fierce determination igniting within—a fire that transcends mere vengeance; it's a quest for justice for my father and a longing to reclaim the love that Celeste and my husband have nearly shattered.

I come to realize that this battle extends beyond my personal grievances; it's a fight for the very integrity of the family I cherish, a fight to restore the bond that has been tainted by betrayal.

Now, I find myself eager to confront my husband and discover what he has to say.

Massimo

As I step into Kastaways, an unsettling silence envelops me, heavy and suffocating, mirroring the turmoil in my wife's heart. The dimly lit bar, usually bustling with laughter and animated conversation, now feels like a solitary prison, where every flickering shadow seems to whisper secrets of my betrayal. The air is thick with a tension that stings my senses, a stark contrast to the vibrant atmosphere that once defined this place.

She summoned me here for a drink, a seemingly casual invitation that serves as a stark prelude to the reckoning I know is coming. I can hardly fathom the depths of my betrayal, having dared to cheat on my beloved Queen, shattering the trust we once held sacred like delicate glass. The weight of my choices presses down on me, an unbearable reminder of how I squandered our love.

I brace myself for whatever storm she has in store for me, aware that I deserve every moment of her wrath.

Even my own men, once my staunch allies, now regard me with disappointment etched on their faces. Their glances, heavy with judgment, pierce through my defenses. Jared and Marcus, in particular, wear their disapproval like a badge—a testament to their loyalty not only to me but to the love I've betrayed. They have cherished Kass from the beginning, always recognizing the light she brought into my life.

They saw how good she was for me, how her laughter lifted my spirits during the darkest days of our fight against sex trafficking. I should have listened to their warnings when they cautioned me that I was neglecting her emotional needs while I buried myself in work. I was hyper-focused on shutting down the rings that exploited innocent lives and on ensuring the safety of the women we had rescued, believing my sacrifices would ultimately serve a greater purpose.

I should have entrusted Asia with more responsibilities, knowing full well she was capable and dedicated. However, the weight of guilt and a misguided sense of obligation compelled me to remain submerged in my work. Now, I see clearly the toll it has taken on my marriage.

I understand that I drove my wife away, pushing her to create something magnificent—a vibrant club that serves as an oasis for those seeking connection and belonging.

Everything stemmed from her longing to create a genuine sense of community—a welcoming space where people could come together, share laughter, and feel a deep sense of belonging. It was a haven she envisioned for others, even as I increasingly felt pushed aside and forgotten in her pursuit.

The irony cut deep; while I was out trying to save the world one person at a time, I unintentionally lost the most important person in my life.

Roman, fueled by rage and betrayal, had already dealt me a brutal beating; the aftermath left me battered, both physically and emotionally, with months of recovery ahead.

When he uncovered my betrayal with his sister, he unleashed a storm of fury that left no room for restraint. He had placed his unwavering trust in me, allowing me to step into the role of protector over her heart and safety. Yet, in one reckless moment of weakness, I obliterated that trust beyond repair.

As I scan the room, my gaze settles on Kass, who sits elegantly at the bar on level two. The soft, amber glow of the dim lighting wraps around her like a cozy blanket, drawing attention to the two vibrant drinks meticulously placed before her.

The cocktails, with their striking colors—a deep crimson and a lively teal—are unmistakably the infamous Heart of Chance. This intoxicating blend, served in ornate glassware with whimsical garnishes, has earned its playful moniker of "truth serum" among the clubgoers.

It's common knowledge that just one and a half of these potent concoctions can loosen the tongue, compelling even the most reticent souls to divulge secrets that usually lie buried deep within. Those who have dared to down two of these enchanting elixirs often find themselves in the throes of unexpected romantic entanglements.

The stories are legendary; many who have crossed this blurry line of inhibition have a whimsical tendency to sprint toward the little white chapel tucked away in the back, ready to make spur-of-the-moment commitments that they may later regret, fueled by the intoxicating allure of new-found freedom and affection.

As I quietly approach from behind, I wrap my arms around her waist, feeling the warmth radiate from her body. "My Queen, thank you for inviting me," I say softly, my voice barely above a whisper.

She lightly shrugs off my embrace, a playful glint in her eye, and leans in to plant a quick peck on my cheek—an unexpected gesture that sends a flutter through me. "Thank you for coming. Now, drink! We have so much to discuss, and I want nothing but the truth from you. I promise to ex-tend you the same courtesy," she replies, her tone shifting to one of serious intent.

With deftness, she raises her glass to her lips and downs the contents in one swift gulp, her eyes steady and focused.

Her demeanor is all business, a sharp contrast to the cozy atmosphere of the dimly lit room, and I can't help but admire her determination. Understanding the weight of the conversation ahead, I raise my own glass and mirror her actions, finishing my drink just as quickly, ready to delve into the depths of our discussion.

How much anger is she going to unleash upon me?

How much longer will she make me wrestle with my regrets?

Kass should know the depth of my love for her; no one could ever fill the void she occupies in my heart.

"Let it out, my love. I long to understand the depths of your feelings, and what I can do to mend this rift between us. You are my world, my heart—irreplaceable. I acknowledge my mistake, and I am truly sorry. I will accept any consequence you deem necessary. But you must know that it was never my intention to cause you pain. It was a fleeting lapse in judgment that I have paid for dearly, not just from your heart but also from the reproach of your brother and the disapproval of my men."

She clicked her tongue, a sharp sound echoing in the charged atmosphere. "Every one of those people were merciful. You shattered my heart knowing the burdens I've carried and the struggles I've endured. Did you honestly think it was acceptable to treat me as if I were nothing? Did you believe I deserved to be cast aside while you indulged in your whims? Did you think my feelings were insignificant? Did you truly believe I would simply brush it off, oblivious and unscathed by your betrayal? Did you really think that your misstep would only cost you a night of tears? Yes, I witnessed your suffering; I saw the tears streaming down your face. But do you have any idea of the emotional turmoil I've endured over the last two years? Not once did you consider reaching out to me and confessing your infidelity! I had to learn of your betrayal from Jared and Marcus, not from you—my husband, who perhaps intended to conceal the truth from me. But do you want to know what I uncovered recently, my beloved husband?"

I have never seen my sweetheart this angry.

But I know it's definitely warranted, and I hope she can find it in her heart to forgive me. The thought of a life without her is unbearable.

"Tell me, my love, what did you uncover?" I inquire, feeling her penetrating gaze clawing at the very depths of my soul.

"Corey did some digging," she responds, her voice steady but laced with a simmering anger. "Not only did you betray me with one woman, but you plotted to betray me with many more. Corey managed to hack into your calendar and forward it to me. You were careless enough to list their names and the times you planned to meet them. Do you realize that's why I had Jared and Marcus fabricate excuses for your absences? But that's not even the worst part. The most painful revelation is that my stepmother orchestrated this entire disaster. She was paying women to seduce you, all to destroy our marriage. She wanted us to endure the same torment she experienced when her own marriage crumbled due to her missteps. And you fell right into her trap. She was there last night, reveling in the cruel spectacle. She took pleasure in your anguish and Connor's delight. I know what Roman did to you, and honestly, I don't think it was nearly enough. But I'm not here to inflict further pain, either physically or emotionally; I simply want you to grasp the depth of my hurt. You've cast me back into a dark place I thought I'd escaped. I feel unwanted, as if I'm merely a shadow of your desires. I feel like a mere accessory for you, something you can discard without a second thought. I feel like I need to retreat into hiding, as I'm not the strong queen I aspired to be. I feel like a servant here, existing solely for your gratification."

What?

"Is that truly how I have made her feel?"

She stands before me, shattered, her metaphorical crown slipping from her brow.

"My love, that's not how I see you. You are my everything. Always and forever."

She lets out a scoff, her bitterness cutting through the air like a blade. "Yeah, right! I wasn't your love when you were entwined with other women, sharing laughter and intimacy while I waited in silence. I wasn't your love when you neglected me, leaving responsibilities that my own capable team could manage for me to handle all alone, feeling every day like I was drowning in a sea of your indifference. I wasn't your love when work took precedence over our precious moments together, leaving me to sit alone in restaurants, staring at the empty seat across from me, wondering when you would finally prioritize us. I wasn't your love when I had to craft elaborate excuses for your absence to your son, who looked up at me with innocent eyes, repeatedly asking where you were and when you'd be home. I wasn't your love when I lay awake at night, yearning for you to simply hold me close and reassure me, feeling like a ghost in our own home. I wasn't your love when you barely acknowledged me during our conversations, your gaze wandering to your phone or the random TV shows we never cared to watch together. I wasn't your love when I poured my heart into cooking dinner for you each night, creating meals with the hope that you'd appreciate them, only for you to stroll in hours late to find your plate cold and untouched. Massimo, I haven't felt like your love for nearly four long years. That's why I left and created Kastaways, a sanctuary for those who never want to experience the heartache I endured. I returned to you, giving you a chance to come clean and to make amends, to rebuild what we once had. Do you even feel remorse for what you've done? Or, given the chance, would you choose to betray me all over again?"

Did I really do all that? It's hard to wrap my head around the reality of it all.

As I look into Kass's eyes, a mixture of anger and hurt reflects back at me. It feels like she thinks I mean nothing to her anymore. The weight of my neglect for both her and our son hits me like a ton of bricks, and I hadn't even realized how far I had fallen until this moment.

How have I become such a terrible husband and father? It's gut-wrenching to think about the countless times I chose work over family, chasing after ambitions while my loved ones slipped further away from me.

Kass slides another drink toward me, her face a mask of indifference as she chugs hers down in one swift motion. I mimic her action, gulping my drink back with an urgency that does nothing to ease the tightness in my chest.

"Baby, please tell me what I can do. How can I make it up to you? I swear I'll change! I'll do anything you want! I promise I'll do everything for you! Just guide me, my love!" My voice cracks under the weight of my desperation, and I feel the hot tears streaming down my face.

Why did I let this happen? Why did I allow lust to cloud my judgment and jeopardize my family? Why didn't I prioritize my marriage, the very foundation of my life?

Kass's expression doesn't soften. Instead, she slides a stack of papers across the table to me with an almost clinical detachment.

"Sign on the dotted line. I want nothing from you. Let's end this." Her voice is steady, but the pain hidden beneath it is palpable. "I'll stay here in Mississippi, and you can go back to Chicago. I have enough money saved up for years to come, so I don't need financial support from you. I'll come home for the holidays to be with our son, but I can't promise I'll ever love you the way I did before. Your betrayal hurt me too deeply. I will handle Celeste and Roy on my own. If one day I need your help, I'll ask, but please understand, I won't come back to you just because you're sorry."

Divorce papers! The finality of it all sinks in, and disbelief courses through my veins. She can't truly believe I would sign these. How did it come to this?

"Kass, no! We can't get divorced! I made a mistake, and I regret it deeply, but I need you—the Bratva women need you! Please, for the sake of everything we built together, think this through!"

She gazes at me as if I've sprouted a second head, her expression a mixture of disbelief and steely resolve. "I will always stand by the Bratva women, but you? I can no longer do this. Corey has sent all the information to Jared and Marcus. They are the only ones who possess the complete truth, and I intend for it to remain that way. You can tell everyone else whatever narrative you wish, but we are over. Sign the papers. If you refuse, I'll take you to court and expose the evidence of your infidelity."

This is precisely why she reigns as my queen.

She knows what she wants, and she seizes it with unwavering determination.

With a heavy heart, I sign on the dotted line.

"Your word is law, my Queen."

Kass

He signed the papers, his ink leaving a permanent mark on our lives.

This moment signifies the end of an era that once brimmed with shared dreams and endless possibilities. What will I do now that our chapter has come to a close?

I'm distraught, grappling with the reality that he actually went along with it; I had hoped for a struggle, a sign that he still cared enough to fight for what we built together.

In those final moments, he barely glanced up from the table, asked only two questions about the process, and acquiesced to everything without hesitation. Do I truly mean so little to him that he would let go so easily?

What will my life be like now, in this unexpected void?

Will I still embody the strong, confident woman he helped me become, or will I shrink back into the timid doormat I once was, the one afraid to voice her needs or desires?

Tori

What the hell is happening?

The King and Queen of the Bratva are getting a divorce!

I walked into my office to grab my jacket when I overheard Kass and Massimo talking in hushed tones. The tension in the room was palpable.

He cheated on her? Unbelievable!

That's the reason she requested that performance with Connor! A public declaration of her rebellion, a way to hit back at him.

If she hadn't already dealt with him in her own way, I would have made sure he regretted it.

"Thank you for understanding, my King," Kass said, her voice steady but laced with sadness. "I will get these documents filed right away. You are free of me." She handed him his ring back, her fingers lingering over the cool metal for just a moment. "As for the necklace, I won't return it just yet. I need to hold onto something that makes me feel safe for a little while. But I won't ask for anything more. Have a nice life, boss man."

Massimo sighed deeply, the weight of his responsibilities evident on his face. "Your wish is my command, but don't think for a second that I'll let you simply vanish from my life. I'll be returning to Chicago for now, but mark my words, I will come back for you. No matter what, this is not the end of us, my Queen."

Kass's expression hardened, resolve shining in her eyes. "I stopped being your Queen the moment you chose to be with another woman. This chapter is closed. Goodbye."

Massimo leaves the club, cursing under his breath.

I walk out to the bar and slip my arms around Kass, "You will always be my queen. Why did you tell us he cheated on you? We could have hurt him so much more!"

I take a seat next to her at the bar, her sad eyes penetrating my heart.

"There's nothing else to do. Roman beat the crap out of him when he found out. This has to stay secret. I will not put Massimo or the Bratva women at risk. You are now one of the few who know the truth. I didn't want this to spread to his men. Have Corey delete the footage of today. I am so embarrassed that this happened, but I will get through it. Can I ask you for a favor?"

"Of course, anything you need, my Queen."

She smirks, "It seems I am staying in Mississippi, so I need something to occupy my time. Can I please have a job?"

"Kass, are you serious? Don't toy with me like this! This is your club, not mine! Yes, you signed it over to me, but this is your baby, your vision come to life! I'll make sure you're on the books; you will always have complete authority here! Forget about that jerk! You deserve the world, and my crew and I will do everything in our power to ensure you get it!"

She lets out a deep sigh, resting her head gently on my shoulder, the weight of her worries pressing down on us both. "Thank you, Tore. I'm sorry I wasn't completely honest about why I needed Connor."

I hope she doesn't think I'm angry!

"Kass, stop it! There's no reason to apologize. You know Connor and I are open to sharing. Honestly, it was a relief for me. Being almost four months pregnant, my libido feels like a distant memory. I know he enjoyed it, and I'm genuinely glad you did too. Never apologize for this; we all understood what we were stepping into."

Tears streamed down her cheeks, glistening in the dim light of the room as she hastily wiped them away with the back of her hand. Her voice trembled for a brief moment before she regained her composure, a fierce determination shining in her eyes. "Thank you," she said, her tone growing cold and steely. "Now, can we put aside the sentimental nonsense and focus on the plan for Celete and Roy's demise?"

There she stood once more—the formidable queen we all know and adore, poised to reclaim her throne with a blend of calculated precision and an unwavering resolve that could intimidate even the most hardened hearts.

"Yes, my Queen. Fill me in! We will resolve this matter before they even have a chance to blink!" My voice was urgent, tinged with excitement and determination.

With a casual shrug, she replied, "I had you create a fake invite for Celeste. That will be her ticket to the dungeon, where she'll be safely locked away. As for Roy, Corey is conducting a thorough background check on him to see how it all unfolds. I will need you to secure my position in the dungeon with Celeste; I'll take care of her. Once she's dealt with, we can figure out what Corey intends to do. Celeste is coming tonight—are you ready?"

I nodded vigorously, my heart racing. "Absolutely, but you must keep your phone close at hand. I'll be monitoring the cameras the entire time. We won't lose you—not now, not ever. Enjoy yourself, but I expect you to stay alive for at least another decade!"

She chuckled, a sound rich with mischief, "Fine, I'll allow you to play the protective role this time, mama bear."

Damn right, she will!

Kastaways will remain a sanctuary of love and safety, especially when we're not entangled in the chaotic webs of Bratva business.

18

Corey

TWO MONTHS LATER...

The ruthless Queen has struck again: Celeste has gone missing.

Well, not exactly.

She is currently enjoying an extended vacation... with the fishes, if you know what I mean.

Celeste was not only behind Massimo's shocking infidelity but also betrayed Kass's dad in a way that shattered their family. Her deceit ran deep: she had manipulated relationships and trust for her own gain. To make matters worse, she hacked into the security system I had meticulously put in place, wiring herself thousands of dollars from various accounts.

Needless to say, I'm grateful I uncovered her treachery the night of Kass's carefully orchestrated plan to expose her; otherwise, Celeste might still be leading her charade, blissfully unaware of her impending downfall.

Roy is oblivious to it all, he has been back to the club multiple times, each time with a different woman to play and watch the performances.

Since his arrival, he has been persistently seeking my wife's attention, often lingering in her vicinity and making casual remarks intended to charm.

However, Tori, Kass, and I have formed a united front, ensuring he doesn't get too close or too comfortable.

So far, he has refrained from making any overt advances, but I remain vigilant, keeping a watchful eye on him at all times. I know that any lapse in my vigilance could allow him to cross a line that I can't allow. The tension in our shared spaces crackles like static electricity, a warning that I must remain alert to even the subtlest changes in his behavior.

Shannon and I have been married for two months and one week, and so far, it has been pure bliss. She has opened up to me fully, peeling back the layers of her past like the pages of a cherished book, and I feel like I know almost everything about her—the quirks, the dreams, and the shadows that linger.

During one late-night conversation, over cups of chamomile tea, she revealed the heartbreaking truth about the prominent scar that runs jagged down her leg.

The story behind it is both horrifying and tragic: Roy, her former partner, inflicted that scar simply because she dared to wear a skirt that he deemed too short. In an act of cruelty that still makes my blood boil, he cut her open from the top of her hip down to her ankle, as if trying to erase her right to express herself, leaving a physical reminder of his control. He did this so she would never again have the courage to show that much skin.

If it were up to me, his actions would have consequences far beyond what the law could provide, a fate where he would be swimming with the fish, an expression of how deeply I want to protect her. But my kind-hearted wife has decided that she wants to leave her past behind, to forgive and spare her abuser, an inclination that both perplexes and inspires me.

In her eyes, there is a fierce determination to find peace, even if it means carrying the weight of that scar, both physically and emotionally.

I will never allow him or anyone to harm my Rose like that again.

After weeks of digging, I finally have the results back from the comprehensive background check I ran on Roy. The revelations are shocking, to say the least!

It turns out he was Cornelis's loyal minion all along, entangled in a web of deceit and crime.

We got him!

I can already imagine the look on Connor's face when he hears that we've uncovered his dad's former partner in crime. This revelation not only brings us closer to justice for Rose, but it also makes the prospect of revenge even sweeter.

Shannon

Marriage—who would have thought that I would find such profound happiness in this new chapter of my life? It feels like a beautiful do-over, a chance to embrace love and companionship fully after years of uncertainty and heartache. Each day with my partner feels like a celebration, a shared journey where laughter and trust weave seamlessly into our lives.

My experience with Roy was undeniably challenging; it was a trial that tested my emotional limits and forced me to confront aspects of myself I had long neglected. I remember the nights filled with anxiety, where I questioned my worth and wondered if I would ever escape the cycles of conflict and sorrow.

That toxic relationship drained my spirit, yet it ultimately became a poignant lesson in resilience.

After enduring that painful chapter, I have gained a clearer understanding of what I genuinely deserve—a love that lifts me up rather than weighs me down. I refuse to ever find myself in a situation filled with abuse and manipulation again, and I now recognize the signs I missed before.

Those experiences, while excruciating, have shaped me into a stronger individual—one who now values healthy communication and mutual respect above all else. I've learned that love should be a sanctuary, where we both feel safe to express our fears and dreams without judgment or fear.

This journey of self-discovery has unveiled a profound truth: I truly matter, and I wholeheartedly deserve to pursue happiness and embrace a love that nurtures my growth.

In this new partnership, I feel empowered and cherished, ready to face whatever life may bring our way.

Corey King truly embodies his name; he is nothing short of a king.

He rules over my heart, consistently reminding me of his deep care through thoughtful gestures that never fail to woo me.

He understands me better than I comprehend myself, intuitively grasping my desires and dreams.

Each time he arrives, he brings a stunning bouquet of pristine white roses, with a vibrant orange rose nestled at the center, a perfect symbol of our unique bond. He ensures that wherever we find ourselves, be it my cozy home or his charming hotel room, every corner is filled with my favorite indulgences: creamy hazelnut spread and decadent hazelnut-crusted chocolate, just waiting to delight my senses.

While we haven't fully taken the next step to move in together yet, we make it a point to spend every night side by side, whether it's at my place or his.

Kass was refreshingly candid about her actions toward Celeste, offering to care for Roy with the same compassion Corey had shown.

Yet, I find myself reluctant to assume the roles of judge and jury, unless the circumstances become truly dire.

Do I consider all the trials I endured at the hands of Roy to be dire?

Absolutely.

Do I believe that he deserves to pay with his life for the atrocities he inflicted upon me?

Not at all.

I wish to extend him the benefit of the doubt. Perhaps my actions may have inadvertently triggered his behavior, and maybe, just maybe, he has never inflicted harm on anyone else.

I firmly believe that everyone merits a genuine opportunity to seek forgiveness.

Do I forgive Roy?

Yes, I harbor no resentment toward him, especially now that I have found joy.

Will Roy ever confront the repercussions of his actions against me or others?

I genuinely hope for a brighter future for him. I long for him to have undergone a transformation, to embrace his own joy, just as I have found with Corey by my side.

Every individual is worthy of experiencing love and happiness.

Every person deserves the opportunity to flourish and make the most of their life.

Without Kass's unwavering support, I would have remained trapped in a cycle of pain, a mere punching bag for the turmoil in my life.

I felt an overwhelming need to be saved, burdened by the belief that I deserved nothing better—a mindset that allowed the abuse and manipulation I faced to persist.

But Kass illuminated my path, revealing that love manifests in countless forms.

Love can blossom in friendships or take root in romantic relationships.

No matter the circumstances or the shape one takes in life, every individual deserves to be embraced with love and treated with unwavering respect, not just today, but every day that follows.

The phrase "forever and always" evokes the same warmth and beauty as a freshly cut rose, its petals soft and vibrant, symbolizing enduring affection and the sweet promise of lasting connections and that is all I want with Corey.

Massimo

Sixty days and a relentless 1,460 hours have passed since my divorce—a stark reminder of how quickly time can slip away.

Has she reached out to me at all?

No.

Has she even bothered to send a simple text?

No.

Did she take a moment to acknowledge the flowers or chocolates I sent her?

Not a word.

Am I keeping an eye on her?

Absolutely.

I deployed Jared and Sara on a clandestine mission to keep tabs on her, stationed daily at the club where she has taken up work since our split.

Corey may harbor resentment towards me for betraying Kass, but to his credit, he graciously shared the password to the server, granting me access to the myriad cameras that watch over Kastaways.

I have been sending Kass things every day, just things to remind her I care.

Yesterday I sent her a wine glass that reads, "Drink up and put your crown on."

Today I have red roses being delivered to Corey so he can give them to her, since he brings his wife flowers all the time.

I need her back in my life. In two days, I will be back in Mississippi to woo her.

A door slams shut, the sudden noise cutting through the stillness and jolting me from my thoughts.

I look up to see a young woman coming my way—Tasha Ballentine, my daughter, storming into the house with fury etched across her youthful face.

"What the hell did you do to mom?"

"Um, you can't talk to me like that," I retort, confusion mingling with indignation. "What is your deal?"

"I bet this is all your fault, so I'll talk to you however I want!" she shoots back, her voice rising with frustration. "Tell me why we're doing this family tree project in class, and when I dig into our history, what do I find? A damn divorce decree! You better get off your ass and fix this! Look at all the sacrifices she's made for you and for me, and for Warren—you need to get her back!"

Her words hit me like a slap to the face, a sharp reminder of the choices we've made. Well damn, we're busted.

"Tasha, I'm trying my best. But I don't know if she will ever take me back; I broke her trust in a way that feels irreparable."

"It can't be that bad, Dad! Anything can be fixed! Mom has such a loving heart—there has to be some forgiveness still left in her."

"Sweetheart, I know how incredible your mom is. None of this is her fault or yours. I made a terrible mistake; I cheated on her. Now, I'm doing everything I can to make things right."

"YOU WHAT? YOU CHEATED ON MY MOTHER? YOU CHEATED ON THE QUEEN? I CAN'T WAIT TO SEE WHAT UNCLE ROMAN DOES TO YOU!"

Tasha's eyes blaze with fury, and in a flash, she swings a fist toward me. I duck just in time, narrowly avoiding the punch that could have landed squarely on my jaw.

"Calm down! I get it; I messed up big time," I said, raising my hands defensively as I tried to ease the tension. The bruises on my ribs throbbed, a painful reminder of the beating Roman had given me over this mess. "I'm still recovering from that, you know?" I took a deep breath, trying to steady my racing heart. "But things like this take time to resolve. I'm determined to fix it, I promise. In just a few days, I'm flying back to Mississippi to talk to your mom. She hasn't been home in ages since the divorce, but we both agreed it's important to maintain a united front for you."

Tasha's eyes blazed with anger. "You mean lie to me? Don't wait—get your ass on that plane right now! I don't want to know any more about this! You taught me that we women should be cherished and treated like queens. You failed at that." Her voice trembled with emotion, and I could see the tears threatening to spill over. "Fix this before you lose your daughter, too. Because I swear, I will not hesitate to change my name to Carter and disown you!"

Feeling the weight of her words, I could only nod, realizing how deeply my mistakes had hurt her. Tasha turned on her heel, storming out of the room and slamming the door with a force that rattled the walls.

I stood in the dimly lit hallway, stunned and defeated, grappling with the harsh reality that I had just been scolded by my own child.

The weight of her words struck me like a thunderclap, reverberating through my mind far more intensely than any physical blow ever could.

I felt unarmored, as if the ground beneath me had shifted, leaving me lost in a sea of regret and desperation to mend what I had so carelessly broken.

I have to fix this. Now.

Kass, I'm coming for you.

I can't let this rift grow any wider between us. Our love will reign once again, stronger and more resilient than before.

Shannon

(The next day at the second-level bar at Kastaways)

Love!

Love!

Love!

I'm utterly entranced by Corey King!

He sees me for who I am at my core, embracing every flaw that weaves the intricate tapestry of my identity.

He treasures me in ways I've never experienced, illuminating my essence with warmth and genuine admiration.

With an unwavering kindness, he never utters a word of negativity about me; instead, he envelops me in praise, celebrating not only my spirit but also the beauty of my form.

The urge to confess my love to him has grown relentless, and I can hardly contain it any longer.

Tonight, as I immerse myself in work, he's at the airport, joyfully welcoming Massimo back.

Kass remains oblivious to his return, navigating her own cloud of sadness since the divorce; yet, her resilience shines brightly, a testament to her strength during these challenging times.

The club pulses with life, alive with the sounds of laughter and animated conversations that create a vibrant tapestry of sound.

In just the first hour, I've already sold twenty Heart of Chances, the signature cocktail that seems to attract patrons like moths drawn to a flickering flame.

As I pivot to refill the liquor bottles, a voice cuts through the rhythm of the night, pulling me from my thoughts.

"Two Hearts of Chances, please. One for me and one for my wife," Roy's voice rumbles from the bar, cutting through the warm chatter of patrons and clinking of glasses.

I glance into the bar mirror, my heart pounding as I catch sight of him—a familiar figure with a weathered face and piercing eyes that seem to see right through me. My stomach drops. Why did Corey have to be gone tonight?

Taking a deep breath to steady my nerves, I turn back to the polished wooden bar and mix the drinks with practiced precision, trying to mask my unease behind a bright and welcoming smile. "Here's yours, sir, and your wife's. Enjoy!" I say, my voice upbeat to cover the tension hanging in the air.

But as I pivot to leave, a firm, iron grip seizes my wrist, sending a chill down my spine. I can feel the unsettling hatred radiating from his touch—a feeling all too familiar.

"Not so fast!" he snaps, his tone low and menacing. "I can't hand this drink to my wife. Because my wife is trying to walk away from me right now."

Oh no! He can't be onto me! My mind races. This can't be happening right now!

I swallow hard, forcing my face to remain calm. "I'm sorry, sir. Where is your wife?" I ask, my voice steady despite the dread coiling in my stomach. "Did you bring her with you, or did you leave her at home? I can definitely get security to help you find her." My eyes dart around the bustling bar, scanning the crowd for any sign of a distressed woman or someone who might be looking for this man surrounded by chaos.

He caressed my wrist gently, his fingers warm against my skin, sending an unexpected thrill through me. "No, sweetheart, you're my wife now," he said, his voice low and teasing. The delight in his eyes sparkled with mischief, while a playful grin broke across his handsome face, making me momentarily forget my reservations.

A cocktail of surprise and confusion churned within me. Was he flirting? It felt more like an assertive declaration than a playful jest.

"Sorry, I don't drink on my shift," I replied, forcing a polite smile while my mind scrambled to catch up with the whirlwind of his words.

"How about we get together after your shift? Maybe grab some mint chocolate chip ice cream? It's my favorite, you know," he suggested, his tone light yet insistent.

What the hell? My heart raced at his casual suggestion. Did he genuinely just propose ice cream? He couldn't even recall what my favorite flavor was when we were supposedly married. How could he act as if he knew me so well now?

"No thanks, I'm in a very committed relationship. I'm married, actually," I said, striving to keep my tone firm yet polite. "I appreciate your flirting, though—it's not often that a bartender receives this kind of attention."

He reluctantly released my wrist, his fingers lingering for just a moment too long as his expression shifted from playful to serious. I could feel the brush of his fingertips against my skin, igniting an unwelcome tension in the air, as he scratched lightly at my wrist, lost in thought.

"So, what happened with your first marriage?" he asked, his voice dipping into a low, probing tone that made my skin prickle uneasily.

What is he aiming for? I wondered, a flutter of alarm rising in my chest. He needed to back off; he had no idea the kind of world he was stepping into.

"I'm sorry, but I think you have me confused with someone else. I've never been married before—this is my first marriage. And we are hopelessly devoted to each other," I replied, striving to infuse my tone with unwavering confidence, despite the turmoil swirling inside me.

He abruptly lowered his gaze to the polished mahogany bar, the rich, dark wood reflecting the low, flickering light of the overhead sconces. A shadow passed over his features, creating a soft line of sorrow that etched itself onto his rugged face. "I apologize. You look exactly like my ex-wife, who tragically died in a fire. I'm still heartbroken over the whole incident," he murmured, his voice thick with unshed emotion.

What a liar!

I scoffed inwardly. The woman I used to be—the timid girl with insecurities that flared with every glance—was a distant memory. Now, after extensive body surgery and transformative self-care, I stepped into any room with a magnetic confidence that turned heads. I was voluptuous, with curves that spoke of femininity and allure, a far cry from the shadow of doubt I once carried.

But a twist of disbelief coiled in my stomach, a cold constriction as I grasped the unsettling truth: he was spinning a tale that felt all too rehearsed and chillingly familiar.

He knows that my death was faked. What should I do?

"I'm so sorry for your loss. Was she from here?" I managed to ask, keeping my voice steady and masking the storm brewing beneath my calm facade.

He sighed deeply, the weight of his memories pressing down on him. "She was from New York. She wasn't wealthy like me, but I loved her for who she was. I know she loved me, too. Her eyes were her most captivating feature; they always held my gaze and pulled me in. She knew everything I liked and always went out of her way to do it; she was my good girl."

What the hell?

Has he bumped his head?

I struggled to maintain my composure as an unwelcome rush of anger surged within me. He never acknowledged my efforts or any of the passions I pursued during our marriage!

Instead, he belittled me, critiquing my body, telling me how fat I was, and insisting I cover my rolls because, in his eyes, beauty was synonymous with being thin.

A surge of adrenaline coursed through me, igniting a fierce desire to punch the smug look off his face, just to shut him up and rid him of the delusions spilling from his mouth. He is really trying to bring out the worst in me!

Me, a good girl? Please. I'm a naughty girl, but only when my husband wants me to be. The things I would never do with Roy—my limitations, my insecurities—are far eclipsed by the spontaneity and passion I share with Corey.

Breathe and don't panic; he's just trying to provoke a reaction from you.

"She sounds like the perfect wife, as if you had a dream marriage. I'm so sorry it ended so soon. I'm sure that if you're willing to put yourself out there again, you will find the perfect partner."

He smirks, a sinister glint flashing in his eyes as he raises his voice, cutting through the ambient noise of the bustling club. "You would know. Did you think I wouldn't notice? You're wearing your favorite outfit—the vibrant orange tank top that clings to your curves, paired with that cheap-looking black leather skirt that leaves little to the imagination.

You're acting like a whore by working at a sex club! You were raised better than this, and I trained you better than that."

There's the real Roy: the insensitive jerk who has no filter, spitting out words like venom, completely oblivious to anyone else's feelings. His harsh words hang in the air, heavy and suffocating.

If I were still Tara, I would have shrunk straight into the wall, wishing desperately to disappear at the sound of his raised voice. The humiliation would have seeped into my bones, leaving me defeated and small.

But Shannon doesn't allow herself to be trapped anywhere. She stands tall, her shoulders squared and chin lifted, refusing to let his words define her.

I carefully retrieve my cherished gift from Tori, an exquisite pocket knife that gleams in the light. Its polished handle fits comfortably in my palm, and the blade, etched with the bold declaration "Ash is no more!" whispers tales of resilience and transformation. The weight of the knife feels both familiar and significant, a reminder of the bond we share and the adventures that await.

I flip it open and jab it into his right hand that is sitting on the bar, the same hand he scratched me with and the same hand he loved to beat me with.

"I don't know who you're looking for or who you are trying to compare me to, but don't. I am Shannon Warren, and you came to the wrong place if you're looking for anyone else. This is a place of safety and protection. You need to leave now! You're not safe here; every employee here deserves to be respected!" I snatch my knife out of his hand, "You better get that hand looked at sweetheart."

He howls with a tumultuous blend of fury and anguish, "This is far from over, Tara! I caught sight of you with that man, and I recognized the scar I left behind! You will be mine once again! You bear the Boyce name, and you will conform and become my obedient little wife!"

In a fit of rage, he hurls his glass at me, and I duck just in time as shards of crystal scatter across the floor, catching the light like tiny, glimmering stars. He storms out, leaving behind an echo of his wrath that reverberates in the air.

He has seen my scar; there is no denying that he knows its story all too well.

What should I do now?

What awaits me in the aftermath of this confrontation?

I steadfastly refuse to return to him; I will not shrink back into his expectations of a 'good girl!'

I embrace my rebellious nature, knowing that I am unapologetically bad. This Rose will not wilt in his grasp.

He will soon learn to feel the sting of my thorns!

Roy

She will pay dearly for this!

I will take every measure to ensure she faces the consequences of her actions!

No one disrespects me or my family without facing retribution!

I refuse to allow anyone to harm me. What she managed to inflict was merely a stroke of luck this time!

She must embrace her role as my little obedient wife—nothing less will suffice!

Since that disastrous incident, I have initiated a comprehensive investigation into the life of the seemingly unremarkable Miss Shannon Warren.

What I have uncovered, while a matter of public record, is shocking in its implications and connects the dots in ways I had not anticipated.

Her birthday eerily mirrors that of my beloved Tara's—July 4th. A day that once brought joy now serves as a bittersweet reminder of my profound loss.

According to her birth certificate, Shannon was born right here in Mississippi. Interestingly, it details only her mother, Cassandra Redding, with no reference to a father. This absence raises unsettling questions.

Driven by curiosity, I began to research Cassandra Redding, only to stumble upon a death certificate for her, dated on the very day Tara met her tragic end. The coincidence sends chills down my spine.

My exploration did not stop there; I delved into Shannon's property records. Intriguingly, her house was purchased by Kassani Ballentine merely two weeks after Tara's untimely demise. What precipitated such haste? What motivated these actions?

Then, I scrutinized Shannon's medical history, and that's where the strangeness reached new heights. Her records mirror Tara's almost exactly, the same specialists, the same hospitals, with one glaring distinction—the full-body reconstructive surgery Shannon underwent shortly after Tara's death.

It has become strikingly clear to me: Tara and Shannon are undoubtedly the same individual. The defining traits were unmistakable—the hauntingly identical eyes that sparkled with the same fire, and the singular scar that whispered tales of shared struggles.

I care not whether I reclaim Shannon or Tara; one of them will soon return with me to New York!

I need my glamorous socialite wife back by my side if there is any hope of mending my tarnished public image.

Since the tragic deaths of both Cornelis and my father, the elite circles of the city have relentlessly conspired to exclude me from their social gatherings. Tara's death provided the perfect pretext to cement my exile.

The socialite wives adored Tara; she radiated grace, always composed, and a willing partner in our high-society world.

I am equally determined to uncover who masterminded this shocking transformation of my once demure wallflower, for they will certainly face the dire consequences of their actions!

Prepare yourself, my love!

New York is calling you back, whether you are ready or not... alive or lingering in the shadows of the past.

Should she dare to defy my command and choose to remain hidden, I will unleash a tempest of vengeance that she will feel coursing through every fiber of her being, as the flames of retribution consume her entirely.

I will make certain that Connor shares in her suffering, for I will never forgive or forget those responsible for Cornelis's demise. The memory of that treachery ignites my determination, and I intend for them to pay dearly for their betrayal.

Corey

As soon as I dropped Massimo off at Kass's apartment, a knot of worry twisted in my stomach, propelling me toward Shannon's house with urgency. I needed to ensure she was alright after what she had endured.

Tori had sent me the video of tonight's unsettling encounter with Roy. Watching him swagger around like he owned the place, a surge of anger bubbled up within me.

What a stupid asshole!

I swear, I will get my hands on him!

No one— and I mean no one— lays a finger on my Rose without my explicit permission or hers.

No one threatens her, not while I'm around.

No one will take her from me.

Roy may be a ghost from her past, but I stand firmly as her present and her future.

He shattered her trust, but I've worked tirelessly to piece her back together, to show her she deserves kindness and respect.

His abusive tendencies drove her away, and now, his loss is my gain.

I will only ever treat her with the gentleness she deserves, unless she signals that she craves something more intense.

Roy needs to learn his place in this world.

And that place is not by her side.

His place is at the bottom of the ocean, alongside his girlfriend, where he can't hurt anyone again.

19

Kass

Life has taught me that love profoundly influences both the body and the soul, weaving a thread through our experiences that can uplift us or leave us adrift.

Since my divorce, my world has shifted dramatically. The vibrant colors of my life have dulled, and I've found it increasingly challenging to rekindle my passion for the activities that once sparked joy within me.

I used to look forward to pampering myself at the salon, indulging in a fresh haircut or a soothing facial, but now those appointments seem unnecessary.

The simple pleasure of taking a leisurely stroll to a coffee shop, where the aroma of freshly brewed coffee once filled me with delight, has become a chore.

The very thought of wandering through the inviting aisles of the bookstore, where I could easily lose myself for hours, exploring new realms within the pages of literature, has begun to lose its charm. I now find myself enveloped in a fog of indifference, desperately searching for the flicker of enthusiasm that once illuminated my days.

I've come to understand that my ability to care for myself is intricately tied to the love and support I received from Massimo. His presence made me feel cherished and adored, igniting a motivation within me to nurture myself because I was blissfully happy and cared for.

Yet, for the past two months, I have become a mere creature of routine, mechanically going to work and returning home without any spark.

At Kastaways, I flit from task to task, filling in wherever I'm needed, predominantly on the first floor.

This level, with its more subdued atmosphere, feels like a refuge to me. It's a space where fewer couples linger, seemingly more preoccupied with enjoying their drinks and dancing rather than succumbing to the temptations of romance. In this environment, I find a misleading sense of safety, but it lacks the vibrancy that once inspired me.

Kastaways was my sanctuary, a place where I learned to reconnect with myself, a haven where I could help others find their path as well. But now, it serves only as a haunting reminder of the failed promises and shattered dreams that were my marriage.

It's been two months since the divorce was finalized, and during this time, I have chosen not to respond to his messages or calls.

Why, you ask? Because despite knowing deep down that the troubles we faced were not solely my fault, an unsettling feeling gnaws at me—I can't help but think that there might have been more I could have done to salvage us.

Massimo reaches out to me every single day, texting and calling in a rhythm that has become almost comforting. Each buzz or ring sends a flicker of warmth through me, and I find myself smiling involuntarily whenever his name lights up my screen.

I miss him—my heart aches for him, and I can feel it in my bones.

He must sense my longing; my phone buzzes to life again, the screen illuminating with "Bossman." This time, I feel a pull, a desire to give in. Perhaps he deserves a real chance, a moment of honesty between us.

I take a deep breath, steadying my nerves before answering, "Hello?"

His deep, seductive voice envelops me as he replies, "Hello, my Queen. Did you receive the roses I sent?"

I glance towards the entryway table, where two dozen roses—rich red interwoven with delicate white—stand in a vase, their fragrance filling the room.

"Yes, I did, thank you. They're beautiful," I respond, trying to suppress the flutter in my chest. "But what do you want, Bossman? I'm very busy tonight."

His giddy voice floats through the phone, warm and playful, "What are you busy doing, my Queen? I know it's your night off, and I can just imagine what you might be up to."

I raise an eyebrow, taken aback. What does he mean by that? There's no way he could know what I'm actually doing right now. Feeling daring, I decide to challenge him.

"Oh, you do? Do you know what I'm wearing?"

As the words escape my lips, I let my silky royal blue pajamas slip to the floor, pooling around my feet like a whisper of mischief.

"Kass, are you flirting with me?" His voice holds a mix of surprise and intrigue that sends a shiver down my spine.

I chuckle softly, the sound light and teasing. "No, Boss. I'm merely proving a point that you have no idea what I'm doing at this moment."

With a deliberate slowness, I turn and walk toward my bedroom, the cool air brushing against my bare skin. I reach for my favorite vibrator, excitement coursing through me, a thrill of naughtiness while he's still on the line.

"Kass, you're playing with fire!" The warning in his voice is both cautionary and electrifying.

"Why do you say that? Like I mentioned, I'm quite busy tonight." My tone is playful, and I can't help the smile that graces my lips, intrigued by the dance we're engaging in.

I turn on my toy and sit on the edge of the bed, "Am I? I thought I was busy playing with myself!"

I held the toy up to the phone, the soft buzzing sound becoming clear and resonant in the quiet room.

"You're not wearing anything, are you? Just moments ago, you were wrapped up in your favorite royal blue pajamas, but now they've been discarded, forgotten on the floor. You're perched on the edge of the bed, your legs relaxed and inviting, poised to push yourself to the edge with that beloved little bullet. I can tell, can't I?"

How does he know exactly what I'm doing?

"Don't be alarmed, my love. You didn't really think I'd leave you without some form of protection, did you? I've taken precautions—hidden cameras to keep a watchful eye, and only I have access to them. Would you like some assistance in finding that sweet release? I'd be more than happy to help you unravel a little."

Naturally, the big bad Pakhan would want to keep an eye on me. I wouldn't expect anything less.

"How do you plan on making me feel better?"

Massimo

Watching her instantly brings back memories of being a shy schoolboy, filled with admiration and curiosity. She exudes confidence, unashamed and proud of her body, every curve a testament to her self-assuredness.

Kass possesses an incredible awareness of her own desires, fully in tune with what her body craves in any given moment. She moves with purpose, her grace captivating, as she effortlessly navigates her surroundings, embodying both strength and femininity.

Little does she know, I'm just outside her door, hidden from view yet captivated by her presence.

"What do you want me to do to you, baby? You know you're the only one who can really call the shots here," I whisper quietly, my heart racing.

Through the camera, I catch a glimpse of her sly smirk, the playful glimmer in her eyes lighting up the screen. "I don't need you, boss," she responds with a teasing tone. "I can take care of myself just fine with my trusty toy."

Not on my watch; I alone will be the source of her pleasure.

I quietly slip into her apartment using the familiar passcode she always utilizes—my birthday. It feels surreal, this secret connection we share.

As I move through the dimly lit hallway, soft shadows dance on the walls, and the sound of her soft breaths guides me toward her bedroom.

There she sits on the edge of the bed, her silhouette outlined by the soft glow of a bedside lamp. She clutches her favorite toy, pressing it tantalizingly against herself. The gentle vibrations send ripples of sensation coursing through her body, leaving her breathless in a state of blissful anticipation.

"I can bring you to the edge—just say the word!" I whisper, my voice laced with seduction.

Instead of shock, her face transforms into one of sheer exhilaration as the realization of my presence dawns on her.

Her eyes, now sparkling with a passionate glint, draw me in like a moth to a flame. The warm light of the room dances in their depths, radiating a mix of excitement and a teasing sense of anticipation. The air hums with an electric atmosphere, thick with unspoken promises and unfulfilled desires.

"What is the word?" she asks, her voice a sultry whisper filled with playful challenge.

She knows the word—it rests on the tip of her tongue—yet she feigns coyness, relishing the game.

I lean against the door frame, feeling the cool wood press against my back. "Keep the toy inside you until you say the word. You aren't allowed to come unless I'm right there with you," I declare, my tone firm yet laced with underlying desire.

Kass withdraws her hand from her intimate areas, her gaze locking onto mine with fierce intensity. It feels as if time pauses in this charged moment.

"Game on, bossman," she teases, a playful smile dancing at the corners of her lips.

I shake my head slowly, relishing the electric thrill that crackles between us. Kass is no newcomer to our bedroom games; her adventurous spirit reignites a fire that has long been dormant in our relationship, which has endured a two-year drought of intimacy. Yet tonight feels different, as if the air around us is charged with possibility and I sense change stirring on the horizon.

"Is it 'baby'?" she inquires next, her voice laced with mischief, the glint in her eyes betraying just how much she enjoys this game.

Once more, I shake my head, my gaze locked onto hers with unwavering intensity. Her expression transforms into a captivating blend of frustration and exhilaration, the thrill of the chase evident in her delightful features. She teeters on the brink of discovery, fully aware that the answer is tantalizingly close, yet she chooses to prolong the delicious suspense, savoring every heartbeat of the charged atmosphere between us.

"Is it 'Texas'?" she ventures, her voice laced with curiosity.

I respond with a definitive shake of my head, the weight of anticipation thickening the sultry air that envelops us.

"Is it 'fast'?" she tries again, a hint of longing lacing her tone.

With another playful shake of my head, a mischievous smirk dances on my lips as I tease, "I could give it to you fast."

Her grin widens, her eyes sparking with mischief as she inches closer, a conspiratorial whisper escaping her lips. "What about 'hard'?"

I shake my head again, my voice light as I counter, "I'll give it to you hard!" The playful banter wraps around us like a familiar blanket, intensifying the undeniable chemistry that crackles in the space between us.

"What about 'boo'?" she throws out, her laughter a melody in the air.

I shake my head once more.

In that instant, I can see the moment she resolves that the waiting game has come to an end.

She spreads her legs and arches her back, and slowly removes the toy.

"NOW!"

That's my Queen!

With a rush of adrenaline, I shed my clothes, feeling the cool air against my skin as I dive into her embrace, every movement a seamless expression of our connection.

"I love you, Kass," I breathe, my heart swelling with the weight of my words. "You still rule my heart."

In this moment, surrounded by her warmth, I know I have found my true place. With her wrapped in my arms,

I feel an unbreakable bond that will last until my final breath.

I will hold on to her fiercely, refusing to let go.

Shannon

I am doing fine now, finally starting to regain my composure.

Corey has a way of effortlessly clearing everything chaotic from my mind, making the weight of the world lift, if only for a moment.

Last night, I felt the need to touch and hold onto anything within reach; I couldn't keep my hands to myself as anxiety pulsed through me.

When he burst through the door, a whirlwind of concern, it felt like a bat out of hell had arrived, ready to check on my well-being.

Upon finding me curled up in a tight ball in the dim corner of the room, he gently reminded me of my place in this world—who I belong to and the unwavering protection that surrounds me.

Roy terrified me to the core last night.

I can hardly fathom how he managed to uncover my true identity, but I'm reminded painfully that Tara Ashley is dead.

The girl I used to be, the one submerged in insecurity, has transformed into something new; she will never return.

She perished in the flames of that suffocating night, reduced to nothing but ash.

The old version of me doesn't need to come back; she was too timid, allowing herself to be pushed around by anyone who desired to have control.

But Shannon is different. Shannon stands her ground, unyielding and fierce; she doesn't take any nonsense from anyone.

I know my worth now, and nobody can take that from me—not anymore.

Corey is a pivotal part of this newfound realization. He treats me in a way that many women only dream about, filling my life with affection and care. Right now, he's lying peacefully on my chest, snoring softly, a comforting sound that makes me smile.

After igniting a fire within me that I never knew existed, he ensured my well-being was his top priority. He gently cleaned me up after a long day, tucking me into bed like I was precious, and whispered sweetly, calling me his Rose.

Every day, he surprises me with fresh flowers, each one symbolizing the thoughtfulness he pours into our relationship. He knows all my favorite things, from the little snacks I crave to the cozy blankets I love curling up with, and he never lets me go hungry. It's a feeling I didn't know I was missing, realizing that this is how some women live their daily lives—being cherished, spoiled, and genuinely loved.

This feels like royalty compared to my past relationship with Roy, which was steeped in compliance and fear from my side, where love was overshadowed by uncertainty.

Now I find myself grappling with questions. Do I truly deserve this beautiful relationship we've built? Do I deserve this incredible man who treats me with such respect and adoration? Am I worthy of being involved in this Bratva world, with all its complexities and dangers? Do I deserve the protection that comes with it?

Should I leap and express my love to him? Should I allow him to own every part of my heart and soul? Am I ready to finally let him into my life completely, trusting him with all my vulnerabilities?

Our sex life is thriving, and I couldn't be happier!

In the past with Roy, the experience felt incredibly one-sided. He never truly paid attention to my desires; it was always about his satisfaction. Most of our encounters left me feeling empty, as he often resorted to forceful tactics that made me cry just to reach his own climax. It was more about his release than any intimacy we could share.

Now, with Corey, everything has changed for the better. He is genuinely attentive and considerate, always prioritizing my needs and emotions. Every touch feels electric, and he takes his time to explore what brings me pleasure, making our connection so much more fulfilling. It's a refreshing contrast that has transformed our intimacy into a joyful and rewarding experience.

Corey

This woman is my entire universe.

My emotions are a swirling tempest; she deserves nothing but the best.

She deserves the finest diamonds that sparkle like the stars, exquisite rings that capture the essence of our love, elegant clothes that accentuate her beauty, and even all the wealth in the world to fulfill her dreams.

She treasures the delicate necklace that Kass gave her, handling it as if it were her lifeline—a shimmering thread of connection that weaves together the deep bonds and cherished memories they share. The way she lovingly gazes at it, her fingers brushing over the smooth surface as if it holds the essence of her heart, reveals just how much it means to her; it is more than mere jewelry; it is a testament to their unbreakable bond.

I can't help but hope she looks at the ring I had crafted for her with the same reverence.

This ring, a masterpiece designed by Massimo's exquisite jeweler, was made exclusively for her, reflecting her unique spirit and beauty.

In our Bratva tradition, it is customary for us men to present our beloved with a custom wedding ring, steeped in meaning and artistry.

Yet, as I feel the ring nestled in my pocket, I can't shake the feeling that it pales in comparison to my wife's radiance.

The carnelian stone, encased in an elegant rose design, catches the light with a fiery brilliance, but it's my Rose herself who outshines everything around her.

Her wedding band, crafted with meticulous care, features artfully twisted thorns that weave gracefully around the engagement ring, symbolizing the strength and resilience of her and our union—a union intertwined, beautiful, and enduring.

She gazes intently at me as I lounge here in her bed, shirtless and clad in a pair of bright orange sweatpants that I picked out just for her.

"What are you looking at, Rose?" I ask, arching an eyebrow.

"Your sexy body, Jump Drive," she replies, a playful glimmer in her eyes.

I smirk, teasing her. "I'm noticing your naked finger."

With a flick of her wrist, she glances down at her perfectly manicured nails, polished to a vibrant orange. "My fingers are hardly naked; they're adorned with these striking nails. What are you talking about?"

Rising slowly from the bed, I stride toward her, each step intentional. I reach her, my fingers gently tracing the delicate curve of her necklace, a glimmering piece that complements her radiant skin.

"This exquisite pendant accentuates your neckline beautifully, but your left finger deserves an adornment as well," I say, my voice low and rich with intention.

Her brows furrow in confusion, uncertainty dancing in her eyes. "What do you mean?"

With a slow, deliberate motion, I lower myself to one knee, producing an orange velvet box from my pocket. Her eyes widen in disbelief, sparkling with surprise.

"My heart should adorn your finger, but since that's not possible, I offer you this ring to symbolize it instead," I say, my voice steady yet filled with emotion.

Tears gather in her eyes, shimmering like tiny stars caught in the soft light around us. "Are you claiming me?"

she asks, her voice barely above a whisper, a mixture of hope and disbelief playing across her features.

"Rose, I claimed you the night we exchanged vows, without a doubt or hesitation," I respond, my heart racing. "Will you accept this ring and my heart, fully and completely?"

She crouches down gracefully, sitting on my bended knee as if the world around us has faded away, leaving only us in this moment. "Always," she replies, her voice warm and passionate. "You are my inferno."

I gently slip the ring onto her finger, feeling a surge of love and certainty ignite within me. "I will always light your fire," I promise, knowing that this symbol is just a reflection of the flame that burns brightly in my heart for her.

Shannon

He's revealing a piece of his heart; he dedicated countless hours to choosing the perfect ring, meticulously exploring every detail—from the shimmering diamond cut that catches the light just right to the delicate band that complements my style and personality. Each selection was made with careful consideration, ensuring that it reflects not just my aesthetic but also the love he feels for me.

His gestures speak volumes about how much he genuinely cares for me—there's an underlying warmth in his words that wraps around me like a soft blanket, and a persistent attention in his actions that hints he might even love me deeply. Whether it's the way he surprises me with my favorite coffee on a dreary morning or remembers the smallest details from our conversations, these thoughtful gestures resonate with an intimacy that suggests his feelings run much deeper than mere friendship.

Although he hasn't explicitly verbalized his emotions, the subtle comments he makes—like his quiet admiration for my passions and the way he seems to light up when I share my dreams—along with the thoughtful ways he shows affection, such as always being there to lend a hand or a listening ear, suggest that his heart is wholly invested in our connection.

He has jump-started my heart; he is my inferno, igniting a passionate flame that warms every corner of my being. Each moment spent together feels electric, and I find myself craving not only the thrill of his presence but also the deeper bond we're nurturing together.

This could be love...

20

Roy

She has no idea that I am watching her.

I watch her as she walks, each step graceful yet unaware of the eyes upon her.

I observe how her breath rises and falls, an unknowing rhythm in the stillness of the room.

I even catch glimpses of her in the shower, steam curling around her like a veil, every drop cascading over her, revealing the vulnerability she thinks is private.

And then there's him, that man she calls her husband.

I have seen them together, their laughter echoing like a taunt.

She eats with him, sleeps with him, and talks to him when she should making memories with me!

He is not her husband; he is merely an imposter, a shadow in a life that should rightfully belong to me!

Her heart is tied to him, but I know where her true allegiance lies—she belongs to me.

In my hand, I twirl her sapphire wedding band, its brilliance a stark reminder of what once was.

Just a relic now, left behind in the ashes of our past, or so I believed.

Three long years of mourning have transformed Tara's absence into a cruel joke, each moment consumed by a sorrow that feels endless. I often replay the memories in my mind, realizing how precious time has slipped away while I clung to my grief. In my heart, I know I could have chosen to move on or at least searched for her if I had only recognized the signs that hinted she was still alive.

Despite the silence, she survived—vanishing from my life for over five long years. It's as if she had decided to hide from the powerful love that once burned fiercely between us, a love that seemed unyielding but was ultimately overshadowed by fear and misunderstandings. Each day without her feels like a reminder of what I lost and what could have been, leaving me to confront the haunting question: why didn't I fight harder to bring her back?

Was I truly that terrible of a spouse?

No, I wasn't!

She was simply too fragile to withstand the intensity of my devotion.

She needs to shut the fuck up and take what I give her!

She will fall in line!

Tara will be mine until the end of time!

Corey

As I step into Kastaways, the vibrant hum of laughter and music envelops me, and Shannon's warm presence beside me instantly anchors me. Just then, a voice cuts through the festive atmosphere like a knife.

"Corey! Let's go! We're headed back to Chicago right now! There's been a breach at Ballentine Inc., and we need to do damage control immediately!"

A wave of frustration washes over me—this is absolute nonsense!

The last thing I want is to leave my wife in the midst of this happiness.

"Do I really have to go, boss?" I ask, my voice tinged with reluctance.

Massimo huffs impatiently, his irritation palpable. "Do you think I want to leave? Get your ass on my jet right now! It's on top of the club. Let's wrap this up so we can return before you even miss your woman!"

I shoot a glance at my Rose, her eyes sparkling with mischief. She gently tilts my chin toward her, a playful smile dancing on her lips.

She winks and kisses me softly, whispering, "You are my fire."

I can't help but kiss her neck, savoring her warmth. "My one desire."

"I want it..." she teases, her voice a sultry challenge.

"Nope! I just threw up in my mouth—jet now!" Massimo interrupts.

Massimo, apparently unimpressed by our playful banter, rolls his eyes at our unabashed corniness.

Roy

The plan is meticulously crafted and ready to be executed.

I still have access to some of Corneils's connections, including a hacker who remains on standby for my call.

While he isn't the most skilled in his field, he's adequate for my purposes at this moment.

He assures me that their operations will be stalled for at least a few days, which is exactly the window I need.

In this time, I will make her mine.

She will submit to my will.

She will grow to love me, just as I envision.

With her by my side, I will regain both my life and the social status I once had.

But should I fail, I'm prepared to unleash chaos; I will burn her world and everything she holds dear to the ground!

21

Shannon

I t's only been a single day since they left, yet Kass and I find ourselves moping on the floors like distraught puppies, lost in our own thoughts.

Kass is wrestling with a whirlwind of emotions, regretting the decision to go through with the divorce, while I stand firm in my resolve, although I carry a twinge of regret.

My heart aches for not expressing my love before he walked away; the weight of those unspoken words hangs heavily in the air. But tonight, when I return home, I will reach out to him.

He deserves to know that my love for him is genuine and unwavering, a flame that endures. My passion and commitment remain steadfast, a fierce blaze that refuses to diminish, burning brightly in my heart.

Let me enjoy tonight and bring smiles and joy to all the customers.

Tonight, the vibrant stage at Kastaways beckons to all aspiring performers! Whether you're a musician, a poet, or a storyteller, you're invited to share your talent for thirty enchanting minutes.

Come and immerse yourself in a night filled with creativity and connection!

We do this once in a while to give our performers a break, and we advertise it like an open mic night because normally our stage is filled with all things sex.

This gives our scene performers a break, not that they ever complain.

After playing with Corey at the club, I finally discovered what I like.

I was nervous at first about letting my inhibitions go, but once I found my rhythm, it was like a stroll along the beach.

Do I like it rough?

I have a taste for intensity in my intimate experiences, but I always prefer to navigate within safe boundaries.

Choking, for instance, is something I find thrilling as long as I can still draw breath.

There was a time when Roy would take things to the extreme, wrapping his leather belt around my neck, the cool metal buckle pressed against my skin. Each tightening pull would swirl me into a dark abyss, and although the rush was undeniably exhilarating, those moments of blacking out were equally terrifying and left me feeling a lingering unease.

In contrast, with Corey, the experience is entirely different. When he chokes me, it's with his strong but gentle hands—sometimes gripping the front of my neck, other times caressing the sides or the back, where his fingers would trace lightly against my skin. Every touch feels deliberate and controlled, and I never feel a flicker of fear.

With Corey, I feel secure in his embrace. His intention is clear; it's not an act of malice but rather a way to heighten our connection, igniting the flames of passion between us. That mixture of trust and intensity transforms our moments together into something profoundly electric.

Do I like to be watched?

Yes, but only by members of the club. The thought of someone outside this familiar and controlled setting witnessing my intimate moments fills me with a sense of vulnerability. It seems almost humiliating to let a stranger observe such a personal part of my life.

Do I need to experience pain during sex?

Absolutely not; pain is not a necessity for me. While I understand that some people might find a certain level of pain pleasurable in specific contexts, I personally prefer to avoid discomfort in intimate moments.

However, I do have a fondness for the excitement that comes with being spanked. This form of consensual play can heighten sensations and deepen the experience without crossing into painful territory. It's all about the balance between pleasure and limits, ensuring that every encounter remains enjoyable and fulfilling.

Do I have any issues with climaxing?

With Corey, I've never experienced any difficulties—our connection is electric, and he truly understands my body and desires.

In contrast with Roy, I never managed to reach that peak of pleasure. He was consistently more focused on his own gratification, often overlooking my needs entirely. It felt like I was just a means to an end for him.

Now that I've had a taste of what it feels like to be with a real man who knows how to prioritize intimacy, I refuse to settle for anything less. I've learned the difference between genuine connection and selfishness, and I know I deserve better than a boy who can't appreciate that.

I sincerely hope that tonight will unfold without any hitches, allowing me to return home and call my husband. My body aches with longing, craving the heat of his passion and the warmth of his embrace. The thought of his touch sends shivers down my spine, igniting a deep desire that has been simmering all day.

I can't wait for my inferno to be ignited once again.

Roy

Throughout the evening, she has captivated everyone in the room with her alluring presence, wearing a stunning, form-fitting dress that elegantly accentuates her curves. The deep jewel tones of the fabric complement her skin beautifully, while the subtle shimmer catches the light with every graceful movement she makes. Her confidence radiates like an aura, and with each smile, I find myself drawn in deeper, as if under a spell.

The desire I feel for her is almost palpable, surging and intensifying with every passing moment. It transcends mere attraction; it is a deep craving for connection, an irresistible pull to understand the woman behind that enchanting exterior. I long to hear her thoughts, to explore her passions, to peel back the layers of her personality that make her uniquely her.

She has embraced her curves in a way that makes her even more attractive than I ever remember. Though she's not the same size she was years ago, her confidence has grown in tandem with her beauty, creating a magnetic allure that is impossible to resist.

For years, I thought I had lost her completely, and now that she stands before me, vibrant and alive, my appreciation for her has only deepened.

Tara worked her ass off at the club tonight, her heels clicking on the slick floor as she navigated through the late-night crowd. But now, she needs to wiggle her ass over here to me.

After gathering her belongings—her makeup bag—she strides confidently toward Connor, her smile bright under the neon lights. Little does she know, I'm lurking outside the entrance, watching intently through the glass doors.

"How are you holding up, Shan? Tell me what you need, sweetheart!" Connor's voice oozes charm, a playful inflection in his tone.

Why is he calling her sweetheart? A wave of jealousy crashes over me. Is she sleeping with him too?

She sighs deeply, her shoulders slumping slightly as if the weight of the world rests on them. "I'm holding up like used tape. I miss him so much, and I need to tell him I love him. But who knows when he'll be back? I'm kind of nervous; I want to do something sexy for him, but I don't know what."

Connor's lips curl into a smirk, his hand casually resting on her shoulder. The way he touches her—too intimate for my liking—ignites a fire of possessiveness within me.

I want to cut off his hand for encroaching on what is mine.

"Go into the library," he suggests, his voice smooth like honey. "I'll have Tore meet you there with some options to wear and tips and tricks on how to seduce your man."

NO! This is not what she needs. She needs to be obedient, not seductive!

Tara beams at him, joy lighting up her features as she leans in to hug Connor tightly, gratitude spilling over. "Thank you! I'll head that way in about ten minutes. First, I need to take the trash out to the big can in the alley."

"Of course! You know we'd do anything for you, Shan." His reply is slick and rehearsed, a clear testament to his intentions.

Her body presses against his for what feels like an eternity, and I can feel my blood boiling with rage. Finally, they pull apart, but the tension between them lingers like an unwelcome fog.

I am livid, seething at the sight of Connor and the way he has invaded her space. But I will get my revenge on him soon.

Right now, I swiftly make my way to the alleyway. She might be taking out the trash, but I am about to claim my prize and remind her who truly deserves her attention.

Shannon

I absolutely loathe the task of taking out the trash, particularly when the clock strikes five in the morning and the world outside remains shrouded in an inky darkness.

Typically, I'm home by four A.M., but tonight demanded a longer vigil for cleaning.

The frigid morning air wraps around me like a reluctant embrace, sending icy shivers racing down my spine as I step outside, resisting the cold that seeps into my bones. I gaze upward at the vast, star-studded expanse, wishing with all my might for an escape from this mundane chore that hangs over me like a dark cloud, a stark reminder of the relentless responsibilities of adulthood.

Yet amid this dreary ritual, my heart flutters with anticipation at the thought of gathering tips from Tore on how to truly captivate my husband's heart. With each passing day, I can feel my confidence blossoming like vibrant flowers bursting forth in the warmth of spring. I'm eager for Corey to see just how profoundly I yearn for him in my life. I long to unleash a whirlwind of passion that will sweep us both off our feet, rekindling the spark that initially drew us together.

As I hurl the trash into the dumpster—the unpleasant odor mingling with the crisp air—I suddenly hear footsteps behind me, their sound slicing through the stillness of the early morning. My heart quickens, unease washing over me like a chilling wave.

Then, slicing through the heavy silence, the thunderous voice from my past crashes into the present, "You're mine, Tara. It's time you started acting like it!"

Before I can gather my thoughts or respond, I feel a sudden, sharp sting as a needle pierces my skin, its cold metal injecting something sinister into my veins. My vision dims, colors swirling and merging into a dark haze as the world around me fades into oblivion.

"Be my good little whore, like you were before," the voice taunts, an insidious echo reverberating through my mind as I slip further away from reality, trapped in a suffocating darkness.

Roy

It certainly helps that she has toned up recently; I was easily able to hoist her onto my shoulder and carefully load her into the backseat of the car.

Tara is mine, and mine alone, a thought that makes my heart race with excitement.

I'm heading to her house, a plan meticulously crafted to ensure we don't arouse any suspicions from anyone who might notice her absence.

As soon as we pull into the driveway and I turn off the engine, I'll unlock her phone and send a quick text to Tori, feigning a situation where Tara suddenly became unwell.

"I'm so sorry, something came up. I am not feeling well!" I'll write, hoping to quell any worry and divert attention.

Let the fun begin!

Once she stirs from her unconscious state, my belt will take its rightful place, snugly wrapped around her neck, symbolizing the control I crave. The thrill of the moment is palpable, and I can hardly wait.

22

Corey

I am filled with relief as we embark on our journey back home, a sense of comfort enveloping me.

I'm particularly thankful for Massimo's sleek jet, cutting through the clouds with elegance and speed.

"Boss, do you think you and the Queen will find your way back to each other?" I inquired, breaking the silence.

Massimo gazes pensively out of the large window, the soft hum of the engines a steady backdrop to his thoughts. "I'm not sure," he admits, his voice laced with a mix of hope and uncertainty. "I long for her to be mine again, but the trust I shattered looms heavily over us. She could either kiss me or unleash her fury; honestly, as long as I have her attention, I wouldn't mind either outcome. We've shared the intimacy of our bodies, but now we're reduced to moments of silent cuddling, the words 'I love you' hanging unspoken between us like an unanswered prayer."

A shadow crosses his face as he continues, "And then there's Tasha. Each week, I receive her menacing texts, a constant reminder of my betrayal towards her mother. She's furious—threatening to disown me and even go so far as to change her last name to honor Kass's maiden name. It's a heavy cross to bear."

Well, shit, I had no idea it got to that point.

"I am sorry, boss. When Kass asked me for the info, I had no idea what she had planned. But I know she's hurt, but she does love you. She only set up the performance to wound you; she hasn't been sleeping with anyone else. She has been renting out the library playroom once a week, to watch a group of the employees be intimate. I asked her why she does it, and she said it's because she would rather watch people gain pleasure than focus on her own heartbreak."

I watch a single tear slide down his rugged face, the weight of his guilt palpable in the dim light. "I broke her, I broke the Queen! Damn it! What do I do now?"

"Boss, we need to sweep our women off their feet," I suggest, trying to inject some hope into the air thick with despair. "Let's stop by their favorite spots, pick up all the things that make them smile, and we'll go from there."

Massimo manages a weak smile, his eyes still clouded with worry. "It's a start, at least."

Just then, my phone dings, the notification flashing ominously on the screen as it signals someone has entered Shannon's home.

I glance at the clock on the wall—almost six A.M. in Mississippi. Confusion washes over me as I wonder why she's home so late.

She is always home by four A.M.

In an instant, I open my security app, my heart pounding as I check her status.

What the hell?

"Boss, call Jared and Connor now!" I bark, my voice tense and urgent. "Roy is in Shannon's house, and it looks like she's passed out. I'm disabling the locks so they can get in. How far away are we?"

"We're about twenty minutes out," he responds quickly, his tone matching my urgency. "I'm sending them the alert right now! We'll get her; Roy won't take her from us."

He better not!

Rage surges through me like fire. If he lays a finger on her, I swear I will burn him alive! My Rose better not be wilted when we find her, or he'll be nothing but ash!

Shannon

A dull throbbing pulses through my head, each beat a painful reminder of whatever sedative he drugged me with. My body feels heavy, as if encased in lead, wrapped in a blanket of aches that seep deep into my bones, making every movement an exercise in agony.

With great effort, I pry my eyelids apart. The familiar light of my living room floods in through the half-drawn curtains, sharp and blinding, mingling with the stale scent of old takeout and lingering regret that hangs in the air like an unwelcome ghost.

What could have compelled Roy to bring me back here, to the most obvious place?

Doesn't he understand the complex web of security measures that the Bratva uses to protect their own? Their influence is extensive, and I can't shake the feeling that he has just ignited a fuse we may never be able to extinguish.

The weight of dread settles heavily in my stomach, a leaden ball of anxiety as I grapple with the implications of his recklessness. I never want to be the cause of someone's death—especially not when it could be someone I once cared about.

As I slowly sit up, wincing at the sharp pangs racing through my muscles, Roy walks into my room, balancing a tray of food, the aroma of garlic and herbs cutting through the stale air.

"I thought it was only fitting that I made you spaghetti," he says, a hint of nostalgia in his voice, "because we never got to eat the one you made."

I chuckle softly, shaking my head in disbelief. If he thinks a plate of pasta is going to win me back, he's lost his mind.

"That's because you were too busy flitting from one of your many girlfriends' apartments. Face it, Roy! You didn't love me; you loved the idea of me—like a trophy gleaming on a shelf, meant to showcase your status. You reveled in having someone sweet and obedient by your side, but now, with your social circle in tatters and your once vibrant life reduced to echoes of laughter, you're at a loss. Here's some advice: Grow the hell up! You have no idea of the destructive chain reaction you just set in motion by taking me. Ask yourself, are you truly ready to face the consequences?"

His maniacal laugh slices through the air, an unsettling sound that gnaws at my very soul. He sets the tray down on the TV stand, the clatter reverberating in the silence of the room, a stark reminder of the dread that envelops me.

I should've steeled myself for this moment, but my nature—a mix of trust and forgiveness—has always been my downfall.

In a flash, he yanks his belt from his pants, the leather curling like a snake ready to strike, and leaps onto the bed with an unsettling eagerness.

Without hesitation, he loops the rough leather belt around my neck, the coarse texture scraping against my skin as he pulls it taut—his grip a brutal assertion of dominance.

"Stupid Tara! You are not in control; I am! It's time you learn your place again!" His voice drips with possessiveness, echoing in the confined space around us.

Panic surges as I realize I am not quick enough to slip my hands underneath the belt, my fingers desperately clawing at it in a futile attempt to ease the pressure. Each contraction makes it harder to breathe, my words choking back into a whisper, "Roy, think about what you are doing. You don't understand who you are messing with!"

He leans closer, his hot breath ghosting against my ear, and tightens the rough leather belt around my neck, a sinister glint in his eyes—a twisted mix of fury and twisted satisfaction. "What does it matter?" he hisses, his voice dripping with contempt. "I have you now, and soon I will exact my revenge on Connor. Do these people know you were mine? Do they know we were married?" Each question is like a dagger, sharp and unyielding, aimed directly at my heart, igniting a fresh wave of panic deep within me. "Are they okay with the fact that I thought you were dead for years? Do they know how much of a whore you have become?" His words crash over me like a breaking wave, each one heavier than the last, suffocating my resolve and crushing my spirit.

I huff, gasping for air, "Roy, let's talk about this. Please, let me explain! I can't breathe!" My voice trembles as I struggle in his grip, desperation clawing at my throat.

In a fleeting moment of instinct, I gently caress his face in a way I know he used to love, hoping to ignite even a flicker of compassion in his tortured heart.

Miraculously, his grip on the belt loosens slightly, and he shifts back to sit on the edge of the bed, his anger a restless storm behind his eyes.

"Speak! You need to tell me everything, Tara! You shattered me, and now it's your turn to pick up the pieces!" His voice slices through the silence, thick with unresolved anguish and an urgency that hangs between us like a delicate thread ready to snap.

I take a deep breath, my thoughts swirling. Should I lay bare the truth?

What harm could it do?

If tonight is my last, then he must know what he has wrought.

"My name is Shannon Warren, not Tara. Tara perished that night in the raging inferno, consumed by flames that mirrored the destruction of her spirit at the hands of an abusive husband. He never cherished her, always found fault in her, taking her for granted. I reached my breaking point with the way you treated me. You constantly belittled me for my body and the clothes I dared to wear, yet I saw what your little flings sported; it made no sense. You allowed your mistresses to flaunt their figures with abandon, while I was vilified for a skirt that didn't graze my knees or for daring to wear orange! Your jealousy erupted over trivial things!

But the darkest memory I carry is our anniversary, when you turned from a partner into a predator. You beat me mercilessly, leaving scars that run deeper than the skin, and forced me to get you off before abandoning me to rush into the arms of your girlfriend. I witnessed it all that night the way you held her, the laughter that echoed between you, and the contemptuous words you spoke about me. The people surrounding me now know my entire story; they've gathered me from the brink of despair, including my husband. Why? Because they rescued me from the clutches of a selfish monster who nearly extinguished my will to live!"

He looks absolutely heartbroken by my words, as if I've just shattered his entire reality.

"You really believe I was cruel and uncaring?" he asks, his voice bordering on disbelief.

I laugh, a sharp, bitter sound that echoes in the tense room. "Are you really that blind? I couldn't even step outside to enjoy fresh air because you beat me to a pulp once a week! Or worse, you would string me up by this ridiculous belt—do you even understand the deep, angry marks that scarred my neck for weeks? You never once wooed me after we got married; instead, you treated me like your property, devoid of any affection. You don't love me; you just needed a trophy that Daddy approved of! And you're the reason Tara is dead!"

His expression shifts to fury, eyes blazing with rage. "I'm sorry I was so horrible, but if I killed Tara, then I need to kill you too. After that, I'll go after Connor—he's the one who killed my mentor. Tell me, little bitch, are you ready to die?"

His threatening words hang in the air, but I'm unshaken; fear doesn't seize me anymore.

He is the reason I abandoned my old life, and he's about to learn a valuable lesson: never underestimate a woman's resolve—or her cunning.

I keep my favorite pocket knife concealed between my breasts, a small but powerful reminder of my reclaiming agency.

I hunch over, pretending to wince in agony, trying to mask the subtle, yet deliberate, movement of my hand as I stealthily retrieve the cold steel knife from its hidden spot.

"You forgot one very vital detail," I say, my voice laced with a calm confidence, a knowing smirk tugging at the corners of my lips, illuminating my determination.

"What's that?" he asks, his expression a mix of curiosity and condescension.

I take a slow, deliberate step toward him, closing the distance between us, my heart pounding with adrenaline. "I stopped being afraid of you the second I got married! He showed me how to embrace my own strength and become the dangerous rose I was always meant to be. Any last words, Roy?"

His brow furrows in confusion and disbelief, a flicker of fear crossing his features. "Last words? No, you should have just stayed with me and been my good little whore!" he retorts, his voice dripping with disdain, yet I can see the crack in his bravado.

Wrong fucking answer!

In one swift motion, I stab him in the stomach.

Looks like the stab was deep enough; he's gasping for air.

For added measure and revenge, I slice his throat from ear to ear.

"Whose the good little whore now?"

23

Corey

The traffic was a complete nightmare, a tangled mess of horns blaring and frustrated drivers everywhere!

A sudden instinct nudged me to check the camera.

As I opened the app, I was taken aback by what appeared on the screen.

Quickly, I shot Jared a text, urging him to bring the cleanup crew without delay.

"Boss, take a look at this," I say, handing my phone to Massimo. His eyes widen in shock as he scans the screen, taking in the vivid scene captured from the security camera.

The house is immaculate, every surface gleaming just the way Shannon likes it, with the faint scent of lemon cleaning solution lingering in the air. The living room is neatly arranged, the plush sofa perfectly aligned with the coffee table, and the sunlight streams through the large windows, illuminating the carefully curated décor.

But then he scrolls to the bedroom.

The stark contrast hits hard—clothes are strewn across the floor, a disheveled bed with rumpled sheets, and a pile of abandoned books stacked haphazardly on the nightstand.

The shock on Massimo's face deepens as he processes the disarray. "What happened here?" he mutters, his brows furrowing in concern.

Roy is lying out on the bed, covered in blood from his neck to his torso, and is unmoving.

"Looks like she's finally put an end to her nightmare; he grasped the thorny vines of his darkness one too many times."

But the most startling revelation is that my Rose is in the shower, the cascading water washing away not just the blood, but the haunting memories of his atrocities.

"She's truly remarkable; she's come into her own, transformed. Go in there, comfort her, help her get dressed, and when Jared arrives, we'll handle the rest."

I nod, the weight of the moment settling in. "Yes, boss."

Shannon

As I step out of the steamy, foggy shower, I am enveloped by the intoxicating scent of musk mingling with the salty undertones of the ocean breeze that wafts through the cracked window. That aroma drives me wild, a remembrance of sun-soaked days and sultry nights.

"My Rose, are you okay?" Corey's voice pulls me from my reverie, filled with genuine concern.

I catch my reflection in the mirror, wincing at the sight of the deep bruise blossoming on my neck, a painful reminder of the chaos that just unfolded.

"Physically, no. But mentally, I am free at last. Can we please get out of here?" I respond, trying to mask my vulnerability with a brave smile.

Corey steps closer, helping me slip into my bright orange leggings, the fabric snug against my skin, followed by a simple black t-shirt that clings just enough to feel comfortable.

"I'll take you wherever you want to go. Massimo has the clean-up crew on standby," he assures me, his eyes reflecting a mixture of admiration and protectiveness.

I shrug, letting out a bittersweet laugh, "I guess I'm one of the big bad Bratva women now." The words taste foreign but powerful on my tongue.

He gently caresses my head, his fingers running through my damp hair. "You've been one since the day we exchanged our vows, which I still can't quite recall," he replies, a hint of playfulness in his tone.

I chuckle, a sound that feels liberating, "Me neither. But right now, all I can think about is where we can lay our heads tonight."

"Anywhere your heart desires," he says softly, his gaze locking onto mine with unwavering sincerity.

There's only one place that pulls at my heart, a beacon amid the chaos.

"Can we go to Kastaways?" I ask, my voice barely above a whisper, the location sparking memories of laughter and freedom.

He smiles warmly, his expression reassuring, "Always."

24

Epilogue

SHANNON

Three years later...

Freedom from the suffocating flames of my past has never felt so liberating!

It has been three years since I made the courageous decision to permanently remove Roy from my life, and not for a moment do I regret it. The weight of that choice lifted a veil that had shrouded my spirit for so long, allowing me to breathe deeply for the first time in years.

Emulating the strength of Kass, who once offered me a lifeline during my darkest days, I am now wholeheartedly committed to rescuing anyone trapped in an abusive situation, regardless of whether they are a man or a woman. Advocacy has become my mission; I want others to know that freedom is possible and support is available.

So, what has transformed in my life over this past year?

I have fallen deeply in love with my husband, a bond that feels both exhilarating and grounding. He knows it wholeheartedly, and each day we cherish our unique connection. As a symbol of our enduring love, I adorned my right shoulder with a tattoo of a jump drive, representing our shared journey and the way we have unlocked new levels of intimacy and trust together.

In a sweet twist of affection, he responded by getting an orange rose inked on his left shoulder, a vibrant and fiery symbol of his love for me—each petal a reminder of the beauty in our relationship.

We refuse to be apart for more than two nights at a time, reveling in the warmth of our companionship and the comfort of each other's presence. Our time is filled with laughter, playful banter, and shared dreams.

Together, we have unearthed our favorite escape at Kastaways, a cozy retreat where laughter and joy flow freely, making every visit an intimate memory etched into our hearts. The ambiance, a blend of soft lighting and inviting decor, creates the perfect backdrop for connection and exploration.

Corey has been instrumental in helping me discover my kinks, guiding me through a journey of self-exploration and delight. My favorite discovery has been voyeurism, a thrilling experience that adds an exciting layer to our relationship.

I have two favorite couples that I enjoy watching be intimate, each showcasing a distinct expression of love. Can you guess who they are?

The first couple is our dynamic King and Queen, Massimo and Kass. Their relationship serves as a prime example of how love can conquer anything. They are happier than ever, and Massimo loyally ensures he won't stray from Kass's sight, which she wouldn't have it any other way. Their bond is not just romantic; it's a beautiful partnership based on mutual respect and understanding.

The second couple, Arson and Angel, or Jared and Sara, exude an unyielding love that is palpable. Sara, in particular, finds joy in watching the connection between Massimo and Kass blossom, her enthusiasm adding an electrifying pulse to our gatherings.

The six of us have been discovering our kinks and building our relationships through laughter, exploration, and shared experiences, growing closer in the process.

Kastaways has indeed become our home away from home; the only things we don't do within its welcoming walls are bathe and eat. There, we delve into the depths of our desires and celebrate the freedom that comes with true acceptance and love.

Never did I fathom that my world and my very essence would ignite for a single man!

My heart burns fiercely with his love, a passionate fire that blazes anew with every caress. My body craves his touch, delighting in the way he sets my soul aflame.

Most of our nights are spent in the sultry embrace of the orange room, the very sanctuary where our journey began. Some evenings, it's just the two of us, lost in a labyrinth of exploration and devotion, our hours melting into a tapestry of intimacy.

On other nights, the room comes alive with the six of us full of laughter and discovery as we delve into the depths of what we can offer one another.

Massimo stands as our unwavering guardian, his decree clear: no one dares to touch his Queen. We honor his wishes, understanding the depth of his protective nature, which only seems to amuse Kass.

Kass and Massimo grace Mississippi with their presence every six months, coming down from their life within the Ballentine Bratva they diligently run. Meanwhile, Jared and Sara have set down roots in the South, having received the King's blessing to make it their permanent home.

Corey has broached the idea of expanding our unique relationship, contemplating the prospect of inviting another partner into our dynamic.

Having witnessed the intricate balance of a throuple with Tori, Connor, and Spence, I can't help but wonder: what would my heart do if I were to lose my partner? The thought alone sends shivers through me.

I do have someone,or perhaps even a couple of people, in mind that could really enhance the dynamic of our situation.

Imagine if we invited another couple to join us, fully immersing ourselves in this exploration together. I could delve into what it would feel like to connect with another woman, sharing intimacy and experience, while Corey is free to pursue whatever stirs his heart and passions.

If Sara is open to the idea, I might gather the courage to approach her about exploring something between us. The thought makes me a bundle of nerves, but I can't shake the possibility.

As I contemplate the other person who occupies my thoughts, it's hard not to see them as the ideal match, not just for me, but also for Sara. They embody a captivating blend of strength and beauty that is impossible to ignore, with a fiery passion that seems to draw people in like moths to a flame. Their presence carries an irresistible allure, igniting sparks of intrigue and interest in everyone around them.

Yet, I find myself at ease with this unspoken connection. It's a concern that feels like it belongs to a distant future—one that will only materialize if I ever gather the courage to ask for what I genuinely desire. For now, I'm focused on the joyous preparations unfolding before me.

I have six blissful months ahead to perfect every detail of the dream Southern wedding that Corey and I are planning. With the unwavering support of our close-knit Bratva family, whose lives are deeply intertwined with our own, Corey is committed to ensuring that every element of this special day reflects my vision. From the exquisite venue, adorned with fragrant magnolia blooms and glimmering string lights, to the traditional touches honoring our rich heritage, everything is falling beautifully into place.

As I approach my thirtieth birthday, I embrace this vibrant chapter of my life.

This Rose is not just thirty; she is flirty, bold, and undeniably thorny.

THE END...